"If you have ever wished Jesus Christ, *Rendezvous with God* may be the next best thing. Bringing Jesus into contemporary times, Bill Myers shows us what Jesus came to do, and why He had to do it. This little book packs a powerful punch."

— Angela Hunt, *New York Times* bestselling author of *The Jerusalem Road* series.

"A teacher and a storyteller, Bill Myers welcomes, disarms, then edifies in this tight and seamless weave of story and truth. It's innovative, 'outside the box,' but that's why it works so well, bringing the reader profound and practical wisdom, the heart of Jesus, in modern, Everyman terms— and always with the quick-draw Myers wit. Jesus talked to me through this book. I was blessed, and from some of my inner shadows, set free. Follow along. Let it minister."

— Frank Peretti, *New York Times* bestselling author of *This Present Darkness*, *The Visitation*, and *Illusion*.

"Gritty. Unflinching. In your face. Emotionally wrenching. *Rendezvous with God* is Bill Myers at the top of his imaginative game. A rip-roaring read you can neither tear yourself away from, nor dare experience without thinking."

— Jerry Jenkins, *New York Times* bestseller, novelist, and biographer. Writer of the *Left Behind* series.

BILL MYERS

Rendezvous
with GOD

VOLUME ONE

FIDELIS
PUBLISHING

*Discussion questions have been included
to facilitate personal and group study.*

Fidelis Publishing, LLC
Sterling, VA • Nashville, TN
www.fidelispublishing.com

ISBN: 9781735428581
ISBN: 9781735428598 (ebook)

Rendezvous with God, a Novel

For information about special discounts for bulk purchases, please contact BulkBooks.com, call 1-888-959-5153 or email - cs@bulkbooks.com

Poem *Love (III)* – George Herbert 1593–1633 in the public domain.

Scripture comes from Holy Bible, New International Version®, NIV®
Copyright ©1973, 1978, 1984, 2011 by Biblica, Inc.® Used by permission. All rights reserved worldwide.

Published in association with Amaris Media International
Cover designed by Diana Lawrence
Interior design by LParnell Book Services

Manufactured in the United States of America

10 9 8 7 6 5 4 3 2 1

DEDICATED TO:

Alexandra	Jared
Audie	Jim
Brett	Joel
Chazz	Kyle
Danae	Kyle
Daniel	Megan
Dee Dee	Rich
Devon	Sherrie
Jade	

Oaks of righteousness, frontline warriors, every one.

❧

Love bade me welcome. Yet my soul drew back
    Guilty of dust and sin.
But quick-eyed Love, observing me grow slack
    From my first entrance in,
Drew nearer to me, sweetly questioning,
    If I lacked any thing.

A guest, I answered, worthy to be here:
    Love said, You shall be he.
I the unkind, ungrateful? Ah my dear,
    I cannot look on thee.
Love took my hand, and smiling did reply,
    Who made the eyes but I?

Truth Lord, but I have marred them: let my shame
    Go where it doth deserve.
And know you not, says Love, who bore the blame?
    My dear, then I will serve.
You must sit down, says Love, and taste my meat:
    So I did sit and eat.

Love (III) – George Herbert 1593–1633

❧

PART ONE

CHAPTER
ONE

IT'S CHRISTMAS EVE. Fifty minutes have passed since I last checked the mail—that would be one Diet Coke, a half-bag of Doritos, and a handful of grapes. It's not that I was hungry. I wasn't even interested in the mail. Just bored. And grazing, along with these little excursions through the muddy gravel to the mailbox, gave me something to do. I know I should be grading papers, but I'm only good for so many essays at a time on, "The Contemporary Relevancy of Emily Dickinson," before my brain grows numb.

The pewter light of what was supposed to be day had faded and the perpetual fog had turned to heavy mist—though it's hard to tell the difference out here. I tugged open the mailbox to find the mother lode of junk mail—scores of holiday grocery specials, a real estate ad, one AARP magazine, two going-out-of-business furniture flyers, and a last-minute donation plea from some church I visited once in July.

It wasn't until I pulled them out that I saw the Christmas card tucked inside. My sixth for the season—if you count my chiropractor and insurance agent. The breezy scrawl and a stamped, *Postage Due* with a little red arrow pointing to fifty-two cents, meant it could only come from one person. It was postmarked, Barcelona, Spain. I saved it for last. Best to let anger and self-pity fester in anticipation. Tucking the bundle under my arm, I lowered my head against the drizzle and sloshed back down the driveway to the house.

Sigmund, our golden retriever, greeted me at the kitchen door like I'd been gone a week. His neediness was always a comfort—and irritation. "Like father, like son," Cindy used to say. It was supposed to be a joke but we both knew better. Not that Cindy didn't have her own issues. But, somehow, we always managed to ignore them so we could focus more clearly on mine.

I kicked off my shoes and padded across the kitchen tile onto the living room carpet. Removing our shoes was something we agreed upon but it never stuck—the dark path on the ivory-colored carpet a testimony to our failure. When we first bought it, the light color seemed a great idea; no kids, indoor pets, responsible adults.

Well, two out of three wasn't bad.

Clenching his gooey chew toy and wagging his tail, Siggy followed me to one of the two recliners in the glass-enclosed alcove overlooking the beach. The tide was out. Through windows pebbled with mist I could see the mud-flat stretching into darkness. In twelve hours, it would all be different. The bay would have slipped back in, raising my beached rowboat, and lapping at stray pieces of driftwood. That was the beauty of living on the islands of Puget Sound. The scenery was in constant flux—not in great, unforeseen drama, but in safe, predictable patterns.

I noticed the cat had taken my chair. Again.

"Karl, move."

He didn't even bother opening his eyes.

"Karl."

I picked him up, all sixteen pounds of overindulged, *Special, Prime Cut Kitty Filet*, and dropped him to the floor. Why he always chose my chair instead of Cindy's was a mystery, considering our mutual lack of affection. But mine clearly became his go-to day bed. And at night? Don't even get me started on the under-the-covers, turf wars for foot space. Still, I'd promised to take care of him until Cindy and her boy toy—seven years her junior—got back from Europe and found a place. Ours was an amicable divorce.

I snapped on the table lamp with its patina of dust and started through the mail. Not that I could focus with that card lurking at the back. But it didn't stop me from going through the motions of examining each piece, one by one—a warm-up act for the main event. When the time came, I carefully opened the envelope and pulled out the card. It was a generic Santa Claus waving from a generic sleigh with generic reindeer. The text was equally original:

"Merry Christmas. Happy New Year."

But it was the signature that got me. After all these months . . .

Love ya! Cindy and Buster.
Buster. What a stupid name.

༄

"I'm telling you, dude, she wants you." Sean's words from the faculty party continued rattling in my brain. I remembered scoffing and glancing down at the Merlot I held as a prop. "Have you been out of circulation so long you don't know the signals?" he said.

"Signals?"

"My point exactly."

I pushed the words out of my head and looked back into the bathroom mirror where I'd been flossing. It had been four days since the faculty party and I still couldn't shake them. Flattering? Sure, even at my age. And silly? Like being back in junior high.

I closed the cabinet and started for the bedroom then stopped just long enough to check my profile in the mirror. Even under my pajama top there was no missing the slight paunch slowly gaining ground—alright, maybe not so slight—but the operative word was *slowly*. And slowly could be reversed. In the meantime—I lifted the pajama top and sucked in my gut. I shook my head. Definitely junior high.

I barely entered the bedroom before my mind was back at the party. Sean Fulton—my associate in the English department who sported John Lennon glasses and bow ties—coughed and glanced away. "Here she comes. Good luck, partner." Before I could stop him, he disappeared into the festivities.

"Hi, Will."

I turned and there was Darlene Pratford, late forties, dressed to kill, with more cleavage showing than a Norwegian fjord.

"Hey there," I said, careful to keep my eyes locked on her face. "How are things in the biology department?"

"My biology couldn't be better." She grinned, smoothing the dress on her thigh. "How 'bout yours?"

I coughed. It's hard swallowing and pretending to laugh at the same time.

"You okay?" she asked.

I nodded. She took another sip of her drink. By the color in her cheeks and the watery eyes, I'm guessing it wasn't her first. "How are you?" she said. "Adjusting okay?"

"Adjusting?"

"You know, out there on the island, all by yourself. Holidays coming up. They say the first year is the hardest."

"Actually, I'm doing all right."

"Not too lonely?"

"You get used to it."

"Well, if it gets too quiet, you can always give me a call. I could hop the ferry and we could grab some coffee. Compare war injuries." She took another sip. "I could give you some tips on how to recover." As an experienced veteran of two divorces, I'm sure she could.

We stood awkwardly amidst the holiday music and party conversations. Well, *I* stood awkwardly. I hate parties. I don't mind people. Despite Cindy's accusations, I like them. Mostly. It's just small talk that kills me. The superficial clichés. I'd take a deep, one-on-one conversation with anybody—shoe salesman or serial killer—over a room full of people speaking on autopilot. Which probably explains Cindy's mantra: "You don't know how to have fun. There's a whole world out there just passing you by." As always, she missed the point. I like the world. But instead of mobs, I'd prefer experiencing it one person at a time.

So, there we stood, my mind racing to find small talk while Darlene continued on her own, not-so-hidden agenda. "Rumor has it you're up for department chair," she said.

I cupped my ear to better hear over the music; some rapper's rendition of "O, Holy Night." There should be a law. "Pardon me?"

"Department chair," she repeated. "With Seneca's retirement, they say you're next in line."

"Yeah, well you know rumors." I caught Sean's eye across the room, smirking like Yente the Matchmaker.

"I think you'd be great."

"Really, why do you say that?" I wasn't fishing for compliments, just a little reality to anchor our conversation.

"I don't know. Smart, witty, educated." She took another sip of her drink. "All the right qualifications in all the right places."

"Oh, hey," I said, "there's Sean. Excuse me, I need to talk to him."

Back in the bedroom, I shook my head as I pulled down the covers. Actually, I was honest when I told Darlene I was getting by. Well, on good days. And the others? A few weeks ago, I began feeling a tightness around my chest. I hate self-pity. People get divorced every day. But the tightness wouldn't go away. I originally noticed it when I sat at the Golden Fin Sushi Bar enjoying my first solo Thanksgiving dinner. Somewhere between the edamame and the spicy tuna roll it grew harder to breathe. And things got no better. As the days turned to weeks, Christmas carols began to mock. Holiday wishes rang hollow. Each day grew just a little worse. And each night? Well, thank God for Ambien.

I peeled off my socks, folded them neatly on the dresser, and sat a moment on my side of the bed. Always my side. Finally, I slipped under the quilt and cool sheets only to discover the cat had already taken up residence.

"Karl."

No response.

I nudged him with my foot. "Scoot over."

Nothing.

I tried again but with the same results. Truth be told, his warmth didn't feel all that bad against my cold feet. So, instead of fighting, I slipped them under his massive, fur-lined belly and reached for the light. "Alright," I sighed, "but just this once."

CHAPTER
TWO

IT WAS TOO realistic for a dream. And I never dream in color. But off in the distance I saw a cobalt blue horizon smeared with growing traces of pink. I seemed to be standing on some sort of bluff. Below, stretched a large, flat plateau; black, except for the pockets of fog. Then there were the smells—cool dampness, the roasted-oat smell of dried grass, and the feted mixture of dirt and animal. But it was the quiet sobs that drew my attention. They came from a boy, I'm guessing around six, silhouetted on a boulder overlooking the plain. The light was too dim to see much detail, except for his wavy, black hair, and the coarse robe he was wearing.

I quietly cleared my throat so I wouldn't startle him. He didn't even flinch, just slowly turned to face me.

"Hi there," I said. "Are you okay?"

He nodded, rubbing an eye with the heel of his hand. He gave a quiet sniff and asked, "Who are you?"

I stayed where I was so I wouldn't frighten him. "My name is Will."

"You're not one of them," he said.

"Them?"

He motioned to an empty tree limb not far away, then to a couple boulders. Suitable locations for any imaginary friend.

"Um, no," I said. "I'm real. Well, sort of."

He gave his eyes another swipe and giggled.

"What?"

"Your clothes, they're funny. You don't live here."

I glanced down to see I was still in my pajamas. "Apparently not."

He grinned and looked back over the plain. The horizon was growing more pink.

"Should you be up here by yourself?" I asked.

He motioned to the empty limb and boulders. "I've got them."

"Right," I said. "And your parents?"

"Mom's visiting my aunt and uncle. He's old. He's going to die."

"And your dad?"

"Which one?"

Ah, I thought, *a blended family*. I said nothing more, just sat in the silence broken only by a slight breeze. The boy also remained silent. I thought it odd to see a child sit so patient and still. But as the designated dreamer, I knew it was my responsibility to move things along, so I asked, "Were you crying?"

He shrugged.

"You can tell me. I'll forget everything by morning." I eased toward the closest boulder and pretended to address his imaginary friend. "May I?"

The boy giggled again. Permission granted. I turned back to him and was drawn to his eyes. Golden brown with lighter flecks that almost sparkled.

"You sure you're okay?" I said.

He took a deep breath. "I just wish—I wish I had some friends."

"Ah," I said as I sat. "I can relate to that."

"You can?"

I nodded. "Big time."

"You're a bastard, too?"

"What? No. Is that why you don't have friends?"

He looked to the ground.

"What is this, the Dark Ages?"

"Not yet," he said. Then with another breath, he added, "It wouldn't be so bad if I could do stuff for people. You know, like healing Ben Hazarah. He lives next door and—"

"Hold it. 'Healing'?"

He grimaced. "Sorry, I'm not supposed to tell."

"I bet."

"But doing stuff for people, that's the best way to stop being lonely, you know."

"Pretty insightful, for what, a six-year-old?"

He gave a heavy sigh. "Another one of my problems. But it's so hard."

"Hard?"

"To see everybody hurting. And knowing you can do something but just having to sit around and wait."

"Wait?" I said. "For what?"

"I've got so much to learn."

"About?"

Another sigh. "Feeling what you feel, thinking like you think." He paused and looked back out over the plain. "Everyone's so sad and lonely. That hurts the most. How can you stand it? What do you do?"

"I have a dog."

"A dog?"

"And a cat."

He gave me a look.

It was my turn to shrug.

"Maybe if you helped people more," he said. "That's why we made you, right?"

"Excuse me?"

He started to answer, then shook his head as if he'd said too much.

"What about you?" I said. "Up here crying all by yourself?"

"I told you. Nobody wants to be with me."

"Right," I motioned to the empty tree and boulder. "Just you and your little buddies."

Another giggle.

"What?"

"They're not so little. And they can be real helpful, but . . ."

"But?"

"They're not like you. They don't have our . . ." he paused. "They weren't made in God's image."

I scowled. "Six years old, right?"

He ignored me. "They weren't made to be his friends."

"His friends—God has friends."

"That's why he made you. To be his friend so you can play with him."

"God wants to—play with me?"

He nodded.

"So that makes me like what, his toy, a little puppy dog?"

"You're silly." Before I answered, he continued. "Is that why you have children? Why your mommy and daddy made you?"

"Of course not."

"So, why would it be different with God?"

"Um, because he's God."

"And you're his boy. And like a good dad, he wants to play with you."

"And if I don't want to play with him?"

"It makes him sad."

"So—without me, God is sad."

"Without God, you're alone."

"How'd talking to some kid turn into a deep, theological discussion?"

He sighed again. "It happens—a lot."

"No wonder you don't have friends."

He nodded. "Tell me about it."

"You might want to work on those social skills. Oh, and for the record, you're barking up the wrong tree. I don't have children."

He gave what might have been a smile. "Not yet."

That's when the doorbell rang. Then again. I forced my eyes open to see the ceiling fan above the bed. The smells and sound lingered just a moment longer. The bell rang a third time. I fumbled for my glasses, threw off the covers, and nearly fell over the sleeping dog.

"Atta boy, Siggy," I grumbled. "Sic 'em."

He thumped his tail twice and went back to sleep.

The bell continued to ring as I staggered through the living room to the entry hall.

"Alright, alright!"

I unbolted the front door and opened it to meet— a pudgy teen, face ripe with acne. Her purple hair clung in strings from the rain, her cheeks streaked from an over-abundance of makeup giving her raccoon eyes.

"Uncle Will."

"Amber?"

"Ambrosia," she corrected.

I stood a moment trying to understand.

"Can I come in or what?"

"Oh, sorry." I opened the door wider and she passed through.

"Took you long enough."

CHAPTER

THREE

I LAY IN bed listening to the muffled voices from the TV in the living room. But there were other sounds—from the kitchen, the bathroom, my office across the hall. She was still up and roaming. I went down a mental list of concerns. Wallet and credit cards? They were in the room with me. Computer password book? Locked in the desk. I had no guns. But what about the knives in the kitchen? The last time her mother and I spoke she was experimenting some with cutting herself—Amber, not her mother. Though I wouldn't put it past my sister either, since she tried just about every other form of self-destruction and medication known to man.

In high school, it was booze, grass, and pills; anything to escape the abuse of an alcoholic father and the passive aggressive outbursts of our mother. While I was hiding out with Charles Dickens, John Donne, and George Herbert, my sister, Terra, became the all-school pharmacy. In college it was acid, then coke. As a young adult, meth. And now? She was trying, I'd give her that but having skipped the opioid epidemic, she went directly to heroin. She'd been in and out of rehab at least twice that I knew of. But she was a fighter. She'd kick it. It was just a matter of when.

I heard the toilet flush and noticed the TV went silent. Maybe she's finally worn herself out and is going to—No, now I heard the scrape of metal barstool against kitchen tile.

How many hours has it been? Two, three? I turned to the glow of the radio alarm and groaned. Eighty-five minutes? That was all? Only eighty-five minutes passed since this creature, this half-girl/half-woman arrived, tracked mud on my carpet, and complained there was nothing in the fridge for a vegan to eat? How time crawls when you're lying in bed fearing for . . . What was I fearing for? I wasn't sure. But I already sensed if I wasn't careful, all peace and orderliness would unravel.

"What's wrong with that room?" she'd asked earlier. We were each carrying an armload of blankets and pillows from the linen closet, past my office, to the living room sofa.

"That's my office," I said as I cradled the phone against my ear, waiting for my sister to pick up.

"There's a couch in there."

"Futon," I corrected.

"Perfect."

"Actually, the sofa would be better."

"For who?"

"Pardon me?"

"Better for who?"

"I'll be working early in the morning."

"It's Christmas."

"Trust me, the sofa is better." She gave no answer, so I repeated, "I think the sofa will be—"

She cut me off. "*Fine*."

The message on my sister's phone kicked in: "*The mailbox of the person you're trying to reach is full. Please try again.*"

I sighed and disconnected.

"She never picks up," Amber said.

"Her mailbox is full. What about text messages?" I asked.

"Same thing."

"Isn't she worried about you?"

"I stayed at Jerry and Kevin's last night."

"You were gone last night, too?" I said as we dumped the bedding onto the sofa.

"And the night before. But, tomorrow being Christmas and all, I figured I should spend it with family. You know, home for the holidays and all that crap."

I unfolded the sheet. "Which is why your mom must be sick with worry." She looked at me puzzled. "Not being home, I mean."

"She'd have to be there to know."

"She's not home? She just leaves you?"

"I'm almost fifteen," she said while fighting to stuff a pillow into a pillowcase. "I can look out for myself."

I let the comment go and motioned to the pillow. "Pull it in," I said. "Don't push. Here, let me show—"

She turned from me. "Did I mention I'm fifteen?"

I watched as she continued the struggle. "You sure you're dry enough?" I asked. "I bet Aunt Cindy's got something you could wear for the—"

"I'm sorry, did I hear somebody say they didn't need help?"

I blinked, unsure how to respond.

She tossed the half-covered pillow on the sofa and reached to unfold the blanket.

I wondered if I should take the other end and help or would that be equally offensive? What was going on? How had some fourteen-year-old managed to switch roles on me? How had I become the one feeling awkward and unsure?

"Is there an all-night store around here?" she asked.

"Pardon me?"

"To fix breakfast. It's the most important meal of the day."

"Right. Well, I've got plenty of bacon and . . . but you're a vegan."

"Scrambled tofu," she said. "Add some refried beans, avocados, and you've got a breakfast burrito—*if* they sell lard-free tortillas."

"Um, it's Christmas—"

"Oh, look, a kitty." She'd spotted Karl, spying from under the coffee table. "Hi there, sweetie." She stooped. "What's her name?"

"It's a he and—"

"Hi kitty, kitty, kitty. It's okay, you don't have to be afraid." She reached out her hand. "Nobody's gonna hurt you."

"Karl."

"What?"

"His name is Karl."

"That's a stupid name for a cat."

"Well, I, we . . ." I stopped and watched as Karl rose, stretched, then casually sauntered toward her, making it clear it was all his idea.

Amber continued cooing. "That's a nice kitty. Yes, you are. Come here. You're just the sweetest thing, aren't you?" He arrived, letting her scratch him behind the ear. "Sabrina, that's what we'll call you."

"I'm sorry?"

"Sabrina, that's a much cooler name."

"But he's, uh—"

"He's been fixed, right?"

"Right."

She shook her head in disgust. "Figures." He moved closer, gave his back a slight arch and, to my amazement, started rubbing against her. She giggled then looked to me. "So, if he's been fixed, it's obvious he's just as much a Sabrina as a Karl."

"We've always called him—"

"What a good Sabrina you are, yes you are." She lowered her face to his. "We're going to be great friends, aren't we? Yes, we are."

That had been—I glanced at the radio alarm—ninety minutes ago. I turned to stare at the ceiling. Tomorrow. First thing in the morning. Tomorrow we'll hop in the car, drive the two hours to Seattle, and drop her off at her mom's.

છ

"Hey there. It's been a while."

I shaded my eyes from the morning sun and saw a boy, around twelve. He was tying blankets and bundles to the back of a donkey. A dozen men milled about, loading their own animals. Like the kid, they wore the same style of rough, woolen shirts and robes. Not far away loomed a huge structure of white limestone further reflecting the sun's brightness.

The kid continued talking. "Remember? Back in Nazareth, when I was a little boy?"

I recognized the curly black hair and, squinting against the brightness, saw those same golden brown eyes.

"You always wear those clothes?" he asked.

I looked down to my flannel pajamas.

"Yeshua!" A bearded man, mid-thirties, ambled toward us. He wore the same clothing as the others which made me even more self-conscious of my wardrobe selection. I expected to hear something but he completely ignored me and addressed the kid. "We're leaving in an hour. You packed?"

"Yes, sir."

He nodded and reached over to tug at the rope the kid had just tied.

"It's good," the boy said.

He nodded but also checked the other side. "Old habits die hard."

"So, I've noticed."

The man cut him a look which might have included a smile.

The kid returned it, then added, "What I told mother—"

"When she chewed you out?"

"It was my fault," the kid admitted. "I should have paid more attention."

"We all should have."

"But, what I said. You know, I meant no disrespect."

"Of course," the man said. Then a little softer and perhaps a bit sadder, he added, "We all knew this day would come, didn't we?"

Just as quietly, the kid answered, "Yes, sir."

The man looked away. "So many years of you being my little boy. After all we've done together, all we've been through. And now . . ." He took a quiet breath, still not letting their eyes meet. "Now I must let go." He nodded to the brilliant, white building. "Those priests, they're a hundred times smarter than me—"

"Smarter, but not wiser."

He paused, then continued. "You said it yourself, *that* is your father's business."

The boy swallowed. "I'll always love carpentry."

"What's not to love—long hours, unreasonable clients, slave wages." He threw a glance to the kid and they chuckled, though for both it seemed a little forced.

"I'll still stay with you, you know that," the boy said. "Until it's time."

The man looked to the ground and nodded. Then, slapping the donkey on the rear, he turned to leave. "One hour."

He had barely stepped away before the boy called to him. "Joseph?" He stopped and turned back to him. "You're still the most important man in my life. You always will be."

"Are you traveling in the women's caravan?"

"No sir, the men's. Why do you—"

"Then stop chattering like a woman and get to work. One hour."

"Yes, sir." The kid turned back to the donkey and rechecked his ties.

"Your dad?" I asked.

He nodded.

"He didn't see me."

"You're not from here, how could he?" Glancing over to me, he asked, "So what do you think?"

"I think I've got quite a vivid imagination."

"That's what this is?" he asked.

"What else could it be?"

"You still don't understand, do you?"

"I'm open to suggestions."

He shook his head then turned back to watch Joseph join the other men. "It's tough on him," he said. "On all of us. Every day I want to show him how smart I am. I want to prove how much better my decisions are than his."

"But you don't."

"I won't." He crossed to the other side of the donkey. "Every day I change, just a little. Every day I become less of the little boy he thinks I am. Oh, he tries, but it's all *I* can do to keep up with those changes, I can't imagine what it's like for him." He gave the donkey a slap on the rear exactly as his father had. "But in a few months, it'll all be over.

"Over?"

"My thirteenth birthday. I'll stop being a child and become an adult."

"Really?" I asked. "Just like that? One minute a boy, the next a man?"

"Of course."

"No troubled adolescence, no angst-ridden teen years?"

"Years? Why would anybody want to drag this out? It's hard enough as it is. He shook his head, snorting at my suggestion. "*Years.*"

I nodded. He had a point.

"So," he said, "are you traveling home with us, or returning to your own world?"

"Do I have a choice?"

"You always have a choice. That's our greatest gift."

"Your greatest—"

"Uncle Will." The voice was faint, far away, but it quickly grew louder. "Wake up. Come on."

The boy's face faded as he said, "Stop by any time. I enjoy our little . . ." And then he was gone.

"Are you hungry or not?"

I pried open an eye to see Amber staring down at me—baggy sweatshirt pushed up to the elbows, tatted arms, and her thinly veiled contempt. "It's Christmas. You going to sleep all day?"

CHAPTER
FOUR

I'M NO BIBLE reader. To be honest, I haven't cracked it open since high school youth group which I'd mostly attended to get Sharon O'Brien's attention. But I remembered enough, at least the New Testament, to know there was something eerily familiar about my dreams. So, as Amber clamored about the kitchen looking for "something humans actually eat" for breakfast, I hid in my office, found an online copy of the Bible, and did a little research.

There was nothing about him as a boy—him, being Jesus and, yes, I discovered in the Hebrew it was Yeshua (how I'd have known that beforehand is beyond me). But what really caught my attention was, as a twelve-year-old, he told his parents he had to ". . . be about my father's business." Had I read that before? I must have. What other explanation could there be? Regardless, I was intrigued enough to keep reading but I only made it through a couple chapters before Amber summoned me to breakfast.

The good news was she'd found some old pancake mix in one of the cupboards. The bad news was her culinary skills were untested enough to require waiting several minutes for the syrup to soak through and eventually soften her efforts. So, there we sat at the dining room table enjoying our Christmas breakfast—Amber lost in some pounding cacophony under her bright pink headphones, me trying not to break a tooth.

After a suitable amount of time I addressed the elephant in the room. "So, I was thinking. We should probably be getting you back to Seattle." She didn't hear. "Amber?" I raised my voice. "Amber?"

She looked up. I motioned to her headphones. Obviously annoyed, she pulled them off. "It's Ambrosia."

"Right. Listen, it's no problem if I take a few hours off this morning and drive you back down to your mom's."

"Can't."

"Why is that?"

"She won't be home. Not 'til after New Year's."

"What? How did you find out?"

"She called."

"She called?"

"Yesterday, 'fore I got here."

"She called you?"

"Why wouldn't she call me, I'm her daughter?"

"Right, but last night. When I called, I—"

"Got her voice mail. I was there."

"Okay," I took a moment to process. "So, you told her you were coming here?"

"Of course."

More processing. "Then she's coming up to get you."

"You're not a very good listener, are you? I told you, she's not around 'til after New Year's."

"And where does she expect you to stay until then?"

She cocked her head at me like I was an idiot.

My gut tightened. "Not here? You can't stay here."

"Maybe you should call her."

"But she doesn't pick up. And her mailbox is full."

"Hmm. I see your problem."

"Amb—brosia. New Year's a week away."

"It sucks, I know. But like you said, you'll be out from underfoot in your office all day. I'll be all right."

"*You'll* be all—"

"'Sides, that'll give us more time to figure out how to tell her."

"Tell her? I'm sorry, did I miss something?"

"You really aren't a good listener."

I reminded myself to breathe, "Okay—So, tell me, what did I miss?"

"Not much. Just the fact that I'm pregnant."

"You're preg—"

"Four months. Are you going to eat those pancakes or what?"

Surprised? A lot. Irritated? What past-life evils had I done to earn this?

Luckily, I had the good sense not to blurt out what I was thinking—which was fairly easy since I didn't know what to think. I excused myself, reheated my coffee in the microwave, and retreated to my office—"my cave," as Cindy calls it. This and the beach were my favorite places to think and work things out. And believe me, I had plenty on both accounts.

I popped open my laptop and brought up the online Bible. Again, I'm not a big believer, if at all. To put it simply, religion isn't that important. When Sean and I get together with the occasional cigar, it's to discuss Chaucer or Donne or Sean's latest escapade with the ladies—he considers himself a babe magnet—but never to talk about God.

Seriously, mythology is somebody else's department, not mine. But, considering the way things were unraveling, I figured I needed all the help I could get—subconscious or otherwise. I just didn't expect it to happen so soon. In fact, I'd barely settled in my chair and gotten through the first chapter of the Gospel of Mark before, without falling asleep, I found myself slipping on a steep, grassy slope, and swearing, "Jesus!"

"Present," came the slightly amused voice.

I spilled nearly half my coffee as I caught my footing and spun around. There, sitting on the bank before me, was a man with those same golden-brown eyes. His hair was longer, but just as black, and now he sported a beard.

"Sorry," I said. I didn't mean to, you know . . ."

"You're forgiven."

I started to answer but had no response. The air was hot yet smelled moist and green. I turned to see a stream two dozen feet from us, its bank choked with tall grass and reeds. In the center, under the pounding sun, stood a man—sun-ravaged face, gnarled hair, moth-eaten beard. He wore what looked like animal skins stitched together. And he was shouting:

"I'm only baptizing you with water! But get ready, there's somebody far more powerful than me coming!"

On the bank to our right stood twenty or so men dressed in the same simple shirts and robes I saw earlier. Separated from them by several yards, stood a smaller group, decked out in fancier tunics and robes. And further up the bank, all by themselves, stood three men in soldier outfits right out of some gladiator movie.

"I tell you," the man shouted. "I'm not even worthy to untie his sandals. I'm baptizing in water but he's going to baptize you with the Holy Spirit—and with fire!"

My companion motioned to the trampled grass beside him. "Have a seat."

I eased down, careful not to spill any more coffee.

"You've changed your clothes."

I looked down to my worn jeans and baggy Western Washington University sweatshirt. Trying to sound as casual as possible, I said, "I didn't even fall asleep this time."

He nodded but didn't speak.

"So—am I dreaming, or what?"

Still no answer, he directed his attention back to the shouting man.

I didn't appreciate being ignored and pressed in. "Why does this keep happening?"

He finally turned to me. "You haven't noticed the similarities?"

"To what?"

"Life."

I frowned.

"*Your* life." he said.

"What does something that happened over 2,000 years ago, *if* it happened, have to do with me?"

He raised his eyebrows. "It's been 2,000 years? That long?"

"You didn't know?"

"Time's a relative thing. What's that you're drinking?"

"I'm sorry?"

He motioned to my mug.

"Oh. Coffee."

"May I?"

I passed the mug to him. He took a sip and made a face. "Seriously?"

"I'm in it for the drugs," I said.

The man in the stream threw open his arms and shouted even louder. "I am the voice of someone crying in the wilderness. Make straight the way of the Lord!"

"John the Baptist?" I asked.

"He does go on."

"And he's setting the stage for your big debut, right? The thing you've been waiting for since you were a kid."

"Not just me."

I turned to him.

He quietly answered. "All of humanity has been waiting."

"That's some statement."

He nodded. "I'm about to draw up an entirely new contract."

"Contract?"

"Between man and God. The old version says if you do right, God rewards you. You do wrong, he punishes."

"Sounds about right."

"You sign your side of the agreement, he signs his."

"Okay . . ."

"But you folks haven't exactly kept up your end of the deal, have you?"

"Some of the terms are pretty tough."

He ignored me and turned back to the Baptist. "So— here I am."

"Say again?"

"I'm here to sign *both* sides of the contract."

"Both sides?"

"God's side and yours."

I wrinkled my forehead.

"Is that a problem?" he asked.

"Well, yeah," I said. "I mean that sounds pretty one-sided."

"It is."

"But—what's *our* responsibility? In this new contract, what are *we* supposed to do?"

"Let me."

"Let you . . . ?"

"Believe enough to let me sign both sides."

The Baptist's voice grew shriller as he continued his rant. "You brood of vipers! Who warned you to flee the coming wrath? I tell you, you must produce the fruit in keeping with your repentance!"

I motioned toward him. "Doesn't exactly sound like a new contract to me."

"Old school," he explained. "Under the old contract, John's the greatest prophet to have ever lived. But compared to the new one, even the least in the Kingdom of heaven will be greater than he."

"You're kidding?"

"It's there in your book."

The shouting continued. "And do not think you can say to yourselves, 'We have Abraham as our father.' I tell you—" he pointed a boney finger at the aloof group in their fancy clothes, "—out of mere stones God can raise up children for Abraham!"

The men scowled, began to murmur.

"They're definitely not feeling the love," I said.

"The super religious seldom do."

I started to nod, then caught myself. "Hold it, *you're* super religious."

He shook his head.

"What do you mean?"

"It's the religious who are going to kill me."

"Whoa."

"What?"

"You're starting to sound a little anti-Semitic there."

He chuckled. "*I'm* Semitic."

"Then what do you mean by—"

Cutting me off, he said, "Every faith has them. The rule keepers. More focused on their regulations than their God. And without God, those rules and regulations wind up killing."

"Killing in the name of religion." I nodded. "Like the Crusaders or Jihadists . . . or even human sacrifices."

"That's right, but not just killing the body. Killing a person's soul. All that hating and judging. The rules by themselves can completely suck away life."

I turned to him. He wasn't finished.

"But connecting to me, my power, that's where real life begins." He saw my hesitation and encouraged me to respond. "Go ahead."

"What you're saying—I mean, without rules, anybody can cash in on this contract you're talking about—thieves, rapists, murderers."

"Exactly."

"But—"

"If they come to me, I'll change them—but from the inside. They'll eventually follow the rules, but from the inside out. Religion is just the opposite. It's nothing but behavior modification."

I gave him a look. "Where'd you pick up that term?"

"You're not the only one who gets around." He continued more seriously. "My point is, religion can only change people on the surface, from the outside. And it often fails. What I'm offering is a change from the inside. Spiritual transformation—not character modification."

I paused, taking a minute to digest the comment.

He continued, "It's like marrying the person you fall in love with. People don't marry for rules, they marry for love."

"Right, but without *rules* people have affairs."

"No."

"No?"

"Without *love*, people have affairs."

Again, I let the thought set, while half-expecting him to bring up Cindy and me. If he knew, he didn't let on.

"It's not a matter of breaking my rules," he said.

"Then what's it a matter of?"

"Breaking my heart." He looked back over to the religious elite. "Sadly, most people choose the rules, figuring it's easier to obey rules than grow a relationship. And by following rules, they can pat themselves on the back for their success."

"And judge others for their failures."

He gave a quiet sigh of acknowledgment. "They think it's easier to listen to their religion than to my heart. And by doing that they miss my deepest desire."

"What's that?" I asked. "Your deepest desire?"

He fixed his gaze on me and said only one word. "You."

I hesitated, looked down, glanced over to the stream.

Reading my discomfort, he changed subjects. "But I'm not the only one on a new adventure, am I?"

I looked back to him and caught a mischievous sparkle in his eyes. If he was talking about Amber, I chose to play ignorant. "What do you mean?" I asked. He broke into a smile. I continued, "What do my personal situations have to do with yours?"

"I told you, time is relative. Intertwining." His smile grew. "*Everything* is related."

"Okay—" I took a cautious breath. "So, if that's true and I'm not saying it is, what do you propose I do? With *my* situation?"

"The answer is always the same, my friend."

I waited for more.

"Love. It's always about love."

"Right," I smirked, "even when she's being a brat to me?"

He motioned to the religious elite. "They're not exactly going to be my friends."

"Behold!" the Baptist shouted. We looked up to see he now pointed at us. "The Lamb of God who will take away the sin of the world!"

"There's my cue." My companion rose to his feet. "Stick around, this could get interesting."

"You mean the dove?" I said. "And the voice from heaven and—"

"Shh, don't tell me, you'll ruin the surprise." He took a deep breath, paused to gather his courage, then started down the grassy slope to the stream.

"Good luck!" I shouted.

He glanced over his shoulder and called back, "Luck?"

I shrugged.

He smiled. "You, too."

CHAPTER
FIVE

"ALL YOU NEED is love." Sure. A feel-good, catch-all phrase. But when push comes to shove, it's nothing but an excuse to gloss over the real issues. And, like it or not, I had a few. Actually, for all intents and purposes, only one—how to survive living with a mouthy teenager for an entire week. Was it possible? Of course. I read all thirty-seven Shakespeare plays in one semester, anything was possible.

But this?

And her pregnancy? Not telling her mother?

I mulled these over as I walked the beach below my house. The tide was in. So was the fog—thick and cold—enveloping all sound save the gentle lap of water against the shore and the soft hiss as it retreated across the pebbles and sand. But weather never stopped Siggy from racing into the water, trying in vain to catch some killdeer or seagull. In the old days, before the OCD homeowners passed a leash law, he was free to leap and run and be as crazy as he liked. Now we had rules, mostly set by old man Carothers, my cranky next-door neighbor. Normally I would obey them—if it hadn't been so early and the beach so deserted.

A half hour earlier I had been up at the house trying to address the issues with Amber. She was sprawled out on the sofa in my wife's sweats texting and binge-watching something on Netflix. Since Cindy left, the TV had only been on once or twice, and only for news. The silence had been peaceful, calming, one of the few perks of my new bachelorhood.

As Amber watched, I puttered around the adjacent kitchen and dining area, finding things to do, stalling until she was between episodes. Then, as casually as possible, I strolled in and asked, "So, why haven't you told your mom?"

"Why?" she asked without looking up from her phone.

"Because—she's your mother."

"She'd just tell me to get rid of it. That's what she always does."

"'What she always—'" I tried to absorb the overshare. "Well," I resumed, "that is an option. You do have your entire life ahead of you."

"I've got an entire life inside me."

"Right. No, I appreciate that, but—"

"Shhh." She motioned to the TV as the next episode began.

"Amber, this is far more important than some—"

She clicked the volume up higher.

"Ambrosia, you just can't ignore—"

And still higher.

The way I figured, I had two choices. Yank the remote out of her hand—"My house my rules"—or be the grown-up and broach the subject another time. I sighed, grabbed my coat, and headed for the back door. Sometimes being the adult sucks. "Let's go, Siggy."

As I walked the beach, I continued thinking over my options. The easiest, though the least appealing, would be to put her in the car, take her home, and if her mother wasn't there, let the authorities take over. Child Protective Services, aren't they the pros, the ones who know how to deal with this stuff? Wouldn't it be better just to turn her over to them?

The thought barely took shape before I noticed the sand under my feet turning hard and rocky. Hot air, as if looking into an oven, struck my face. The sound of lapping waves faded as the ocean dissolved into brown, barren hills, dotted by occasional scrub brush and stunted trees. To my immediate right rose a craggy cliff nearly a hundred feet high. And somewhere from its base I heard faint coughing.

I called out, "Hello?"

No response.

I squinted, searching until I spotted a black shadow amidst the boulders and giant slabs of rock. A cave. Less than a dozen feet above me. And just inside, barely visible in the darkness, sat a man, hunched over, unmoving.

I had little doubt who it was and called again. "Hey there."

The figure slowly raised his head.

"You all right?"

He said nothing and looked back down.

"Hey."

Still no answer.

I started climbing, pulling myself over the crumbling rocks, some so hot I nearly burned my hands. When I arrived at the opening I stepped inside. It was a much-appreciated, twenty degrees cooler. I wasn't surprised at who was there, just how he looked—tangled hair, sun-blistered face, cracked lips.

"What happened?" I asked. "You look terrible."

"I've been—" Still looking down, he coughed then continued in a raspy whisper, "—better."

Faint memories from my youth group days bubbled up. "Are you . . . is this where you're being tested in the wilderness?"

He raised his dark, sunken eyes. "How'd I—do?" he asked.

"Great," I said. I crossed to him and kneeled. "You'll do great."

He nodded and looked back to the ground. I watched, feeling both pity and concern. That's when an idea began to form. Could it be? Was it possible I had somehow been sent to help him? That I was here to encourage him? A strange thought, but considering the situation, no stranger than any other.

I rose stiffly, found a nearby boulder, and sat facing him. He had no other provisions. No food and, as far as I could see, no water. "Where's your water?" I asked. "You can't survive without water."

He gave a soft grunt.

"Had I known; I'd have brought my coffee."

He tried to chuckle but it came out dry and brittle before breaking into another cough.

If I was there to help, what was I supposed to do, to say? I was clueless. I had nothing except the wish I'd paid more attention to his story. All I remembered were the headlines—walking on water, dying on a cross, miracles like healing people and feeding thousands of them with a few loaves of bread and—wait a minute. Bread? If he could do miracles with bread . . .

I looked around the floor of the cave. It was littered with rocks—some big, some small, and some, similar in shape and size to your average dinner roll. Like I said, it was a crazy idea, but no crazier than anything else.

I cleared my throat. "Listen, I know this is nuts but you have a pretty good reputation for doing miracles, right?"

He may have nodded, I couldn't tell.

"Maybe you could put that skill set to work, now."

He continued staring at the ground.

"Take a look at these rocks. Some are so smooth and brown, they could almost pass for bread, don't you think?"

He raised his hollow eyes to mine.

"I mean, if miracles are your thing, why not do a little hocus-pocus and turn some of them into the real deal?" He closed his eyes then reopened them. I definitely had his attention. "Fasting's good and all, but too much of it, particularly for so long, it could really do a number to your heart and internal organs."

He shifted his gaze to the floor, his eyes stopping at a likely prospect.

"Seriously," I said, "you can't do God's work if you're dead, right?"

He continued staring at the stone.

Realizing he probably didn't have the strength, I rose and crossed to it. I picked it up, brought it over to him, and held it out. He opened his hand and I set it in his palm. It really did look like a dinner roll. He stared at it, trying to swallow, but it was obvious he had nothing left to swallow.

"It's okay," I said. "You've passed. You've proven yourself."

He turned it over. Then turned it over again, this time slower. I waited and watched. If this was going to be a miracle, I planned to remember every detail.

But instead of a miracle he began shaking his head.

"It's okay," I said. "You can do it. If you're really God's son, I'm sure something like this isn't that big a—"

"No." His voice was faint, full of gravel.

"I'm sorry?

He opened his hand and dropped the rock to the ground.

"What are you doing?"

"For you."

"What?"

"I'm—to serve you—" He took an uneven breath. "Not be served."

"Right, but—"

"My food—is God's will."

"You can't do his will if you're—"

His voice grew stronger. "Man does not live by bread alone—"

The phrase stopped me cold. *Those* words I *did* remember. And he wasn't through. Raising his eyes back to mine, he continued, "—but by every word from my Father."

A chill shot across my shoulders and down my back. Was it possible? Had I just—had I unknowingly played the role of . . . ? "My God," I gasped.

"Present."

If that was humor, it fell flat. I was mortified. I had no idea what to say or do. Embarrassed, unsure, I stuttered, "Look, I'm—sorry . . ."

He said nothing.

I knelt to his side, still searching for words. "I didn't, I was only trying to—"

He set a trembling hand on my shoulder and weakly patted it. "I—do that."

"Do?"

"Reveal hearts."

If that was meant to help, it didn't. I rose, crossed back to my boulder. I stood a long moment, my back to him, then turned and sank onto it. "I'm sorry," I repeated. It wasn't enough but it was all I had.

He nudged the rock aside with his foot, removing the temptation.

How long we sat in that silence, I don't know. For me it was a type of penance. For him? I'm guessing it was necessary just to recover. Any moment I expected, I hoped, to be whisked back to the beach to rejoin Siggy. But it didn't happen. It was just me, him, and my churning guilt.

And yet, as I sat there thinking, I began to wonder. Was I really so wrong? I understood he was doing what he believed God told him and I respected that. But did having common sense and obeying God have to be mutually exclusive? He gave us a brain, right? If this person, this good man in front of me was supposed to do God's work, why was it unreasonable for him to use that brain to help accomplish it?

"I'm to serve," he'd said. Okay, fine. But wouldn't it be more beneficial if he was allowed a few basic essentials along the way—like maybe eating and surviving? If he was supposedly God's son, why not behave like it? If he wanted people to "believe," he should give them something to believe in—instead of this type of—suffering.

I glanced outside the cave to see the sky was darkening, turning eggplant purple. I rose and stepped out to relieve myself. When I returned, I saw he'd moved to the floor of the cave, leaning his back against the far wall, eyes closed. I stood at the entrance watching, thinking.

Whatever was happening, real or make-believe, I knew I was looking upon greatness. But when it came to common sense, could this greatness, could his zeal somehow be misdirecting him? If this was the real Jesus Christ, the "Son of God," instead of suffering his way along the road to some suicide mission, imagine the influence he could have if he came out, made his claims straight away, then continued teaching another three or four decades. The impact would have been phenomenal.

"You're thinking," he said. His eyes were still closed, his voice faint and raspy.

"You're awake." I stepped further inside. "Not really thinking," I lied, "at least not much."

He opened a single eye and fixed it on me.

Busted. I continued. "It's just that—you want people to believe in you, right?"

He said nothing.

"Instead of hiding your identity and dying on some obscure cross—" I caught myself. "You do know that's going to happen, right?"

He gave a slight nod.

"Instead of all this suffering and dying, why not cut to the chase? Just go to your capitol, go to Jerusalem and show them."

He hesitated. Then, after a moment, asked, "How?"

"Seeing is believing, right?" I moved closer. "Show the leaders who you really are. Do something spectacular, something big. Something they can't deny."

"Big?"

"Your powers. Call fire down from the sky, levitate, fly around their heads."

He smiled at the thought, then spoke. "The Temple."

"Temple?"

"There's a tall wall."

"See?" I said. "That's perfect. And if it's a temple, there'll be plenty of priests hanging around, right?"

He nodded, then coughed.

"So—with everyone looking, jump off the wall, buzz their heads a few times, have your angel buddies catch you and, bingo, shortcut to everyone believing."

"Shortcut." He half-whispered the word.

"Exactly. Cut to the chase, get it done your way."

"*My* way . . ."

"On your own terms."

A frown crossed his face. "Instead of my Father's."

I stepped closer "Who's to say it isn't? And what a great way to prove what he says about you is true."

He closed his eyes, taking a slow breath.

"Think about it. No pain, no death. Mission accomplished."

Another breath.

I kneeled to him. "All you have to do is—"

His eyes flew open. "No!"

"But—"

"It is written!" I recoiled as he used the last of his strength to cry out, "Do not put the Lord your God to the test!" Energy spent, he collapsed, his words briefly reverberating against the cave walls. Decision made. Issue closed.

At least for him.

I instantly recognized the phrase and my gut tightened. I must have gasped because he turned to me.

"I—" My voice clogged. "I don't—" I swallowed, my face hot with shame. "I did it again. I'm so sorry."

He closed his eyes and softly spoke, "No."

"What?

"Not you."

"Then—who?"

"Him."

Suddenly, the cave exploded into light. Brilliant, blinding. The rocks blew apart. Walls, floor, ceiling, everything flew in every direction. I ducked, screamed, but nothing struck me. Because, just as quickly, everything wavered, dissolved into vapor and left me floating in a black expanse of—nothing.

Except stars.

Thousands of them. But different than stars. Their light was brighter, purer, almost piercing. And they were everywhere—except above. Because above me, a hundred yards away, washing out all the other brightness, were two blazing lights. But more than lights. They were alive. I can't explain it, but they were two living, very specific personalities.

The first one spoke. I didn't hear a voice, not really. More like I saw it, felt it. As the words formed, each syllable pulsed, creating a ripple of light flying across the distance until it struck my upturned face—soaking through my skin, entering my thoughts, my consciousness.

"ALL OF THIS IS YOURS."

Instantly, I was back at the house—Cindy standing at the front door, tears of remorse streaming down her face. The image waffles, morphs into a faculty dinner where the college president speaks from a lectern, grinning down at my table.

"—with great pleasure I'm pleased to announce the new head of our English department, Dr. William Thomas."

Amidst the applause, Cindy, beaming with pride, reaches over and squeezes my hand.

"—IF YOU WILL BOW DOWN—"

Now I'm sitting at a book table, autographing my latest novel—the one I gave up writing a dozen times—as a line of eager readers wait, stretching halfway around the store.

"—AND WORSHIP ME."

Now I'm sitting in the living room watching a ball-game with the two sons I never had—ages nine and eleven. My four-year-old daughter sits on my lap—so real I can smell the baby shampoo in her hair, feel her little fingers play with mine. My throat tightens with emotion as I watch the boys shouting and laughing, as I look down and see my daughter's eyes, Cindy's eyes, looking adoringly up at me. But even as the words, the ripples of light strike me with my own hopes and desires, I knew they were only an echo, the faintest residue of much, much greater proposals being made to the other light, the second light—which finally answered.

At first its pulsing brightness was weak, but it rapidly grew in intensity. *"AWAY FROM ME—SATAN."* The waves grew stronger, bigger, racing at me like a tsunami. And when they struck, my personal fantasies, my hopes and dreams shattered, slipping away, falling into the void of stars and blackness

"No!" I cried, trying in some vain way to cling to them. But the voice continued:

"IT IS WRITTEN, 'WORSHIP THE LORD YOUR GOD AND SERVE HIM ONLY!'"

The waves continued to pummel me until I was flung backward, tumbling head over heels through the darkness and stars until, suddenly—

I was back on the beach staggering to keep my balance. I lunged toward a fallen tree and barely caught it for support. I leaned there gasping for breath, trying to clear my head. Siggy, sensing a problem, bounded toward me, barking. He arrived, shaking himself, all wiggles and flying water.

"It's okay, boy." I patted his side. "It's okay, I'm all right."

But, of course, I wasn't all right. Not by a long shot.

CHAPTER
SIX

SHOULD I HAVE gone to a shrink? Absolutely. Not that I knew any. But I could have phoned up the mental health guy on campus. Christmas was a busy time with student depression, so he'd definitely be in. And when it came to depression, I'm guessing I qualified. How could it have happened? How could I have slipped from normal, day-to-day reality into some detailed fantasy so real it rivaled reality—and then attempt to destroy it by becoming its arch nemesis, the devil?

Good luck with that one, Dr. Freud.

And why did I want to keep coming back? It wasn't the novelty; trust me. That wore off long ago. So, what was it about the experience, about him, that kept drawing me? It was like some type of hunger; one I didn't even know I had. And the more I fed it, the greater it grew.

I tried sharing my new-found interest with Sean—the interest, not the experience—there's some things you don't share, not even with your best friend.

I remember we were in the campus commons when he broke out laughing then slapped me on the back. "Don't worry, dude, it happens to the best people. Why do you think after all these years we still can't stamp it out? It's just a phase, like the Coronavirus. Who knows why—loneliness, mid-life crises, not enough sex, or, in your case, no sex at—"

"Yeah, yeah," I cut him off. "I get it."

"The important thing is, you'll get over it."

I took a breath and blew it out.

"You will," he said. "And if not, you got friends like me who can take you through an intervention, help you kick the habit."

I gave him a look.

He grinned. "What did Karl Marx say—'Religion is the opiate of the people'?"

So much for sharing. And if what Lenin said had any merit, I was fast becoming an addict—even when it made me feel thick and stupid and in the last case in the desert, a traitor. It seems every time I was in his presence, I came away feeling as if light was shown in some dusty hidden corner of who I am. My apologies for waxing poetic (occupational hazard) but it was as if the hard, protective ground surrounding my soul was being plowed up in encounters sometimes comforting, sometimes embarrassing, and always revealing.

That's why the next three days were unbearable.

No matter how hard I tried to force another meeting, to imagine myself back with him, nothing happened. I tried sleeping, I tried not sleeping, I tried concentrating, not concentrating, walking the beach, soaking in the tub. I even tried a little "Ooom" from my yoga days.

No success.

Had I offended him so much from our last encounter that it was all over? Not that I blamed him. No. I wouldn't accept that. There had to be a way of getting back into his presence, of working myself back into his good graces.

So began my life of humble piety. At least for the following seventy-two hours.

First, there was the Bible. Honestly, how had an English professor managed to avoid reading one of the most influential books in human history? Oh, I knew bits and pieces, but this time I dug in, planning to read every word, cover to cover. To prove my seriousness, I started in the Old Testament and did it the hard way—with King James.

But that was only the beginning.

I did everything I could think of to lower my *sin score*. I cleaned up my language, tried to think "positive thoughts," especially toward my ex. I worked harder to understand Amber—not that it did any good, but I hoped to at least get points for effort. I even began to purge the house of any and all questionable material, including my *Game of Thrones* DVDs, Cindy's stack of bodice-ripper novels, and yes, even my prized autographed copy of *Lolita*. I wasn't so sure about the cigars, but just to be safe, I pitched the cheap ones and stored the expensive ones out of reach on the top shelf of my closet.

Then there was the booze.

We had quite a collection, mostly wine, in the cabinet above the refrigerator. I never developed a taste for it, but Cindy seemed to have an increasing appreciation—more, I suspect, from our failing marriage than any sophisticated palate. I was removing the last few bottles from the cupboard when Amber padded in wearing my gym socks and Cindy's sweats.

"What you doing?"

"A little house cleaning," I said, closing the cabinet doors and turning for the sink.

"So that's where you keep it. I was wondering."

I set the bottles on the counter beside the others.

"Can I help?"

"I'm good."

I unscrewed the cap to a healthy remainder of Seagram's and she scooped up a bottle of Chardonnay.

"You throwing a party?"

"Nope." I started pouring the vodka down the drain.

"Wait!" she cried. "What are you doing? That's too good to just dump out!" I cut her a look and she countered. "Not that I'd know, I mean I heard it tastes like Listerine. But this," she motioned to the bottle in her hand. "This stuff is expensive. You can tell by the name."

"Since when did you develop a taste for wine?"

"Since I started mixing it with 7-Up. Fresca's pretty good, too."

I finished emptying the Seagram's and reached for the Jameson.

"I can't believe you're throwing it all away. At least save some for our New Year's Eve."

"*Our* New Year's Eve?"

"Well yeah, I mean if we can't find Mom."

"You said she'd be home by—"

"I said she'd *probably* be home. Nothing's for certain in this old world."

I paused. Remembering my greater mission, I changed subjects. "You know, you're way too young to be drinking, right?"

"Says who? You?"

"It's the law."

"Not in Europe."

"We're not in Europe."

"And that's my fault?"

"No . . ."

"So why should I suffer because of stupid laws that stupid old people make up?"

I took an even breath and continued to pour.

"It's always the old (*insert expletive here*) who force their stupid laws on the young and innocent."

I pretended not to hear the language, finished the bottle, and started the next.

"It's *our* lives, you know. It *is*. And if it's about us, we ought to be able to vote on it. Not a bunch of stupid, old (*insert same expletive here*)."

"Where did you learn to talk like that?"

"Where did I . . . It's the 21st Century."

She had me there. In my day I'd have been forced to gnaw on a bar of Ivory soap. But now with TV, movies, and Snapchat (whatever that is), the gloves were off.

"Are you listening?" she asked.

"Mm-hm."

"Then why don't you say something? It's really rude just standing their grinning like some Chelsie cat."

"You mean *Cheshire* cat?"

"Same diff."

"Actually, I wasn't grinning."

"Maybe not on the outside."

"Hmm . . ."

"There you go again. Are you going to answer me or not?"

"I'm not sure what you want me to say."

"I don't want you to say anything."

With increasing effort, I managed to oblige—winning me no favors.

"Alright, *fine.*"

She turned and stormed back into the living room for another Netflix marathon. As always, the volume was loud but not loud enough to drown out the clinking bottles as I dumped them into the trash.

"Please, tell me you're recycling those!" she called.

I don't know if bad language nullifies prayer. I hope not, because I let out a few of my own favorites while muttering, "This had better work."

დ

"Hey there."

I spun from the kitchen sink to see I was standing outside on a dirt street of a tiny village. It was dusk. I was gathered with what must have been forty or fifty locals—all standing around a small stone and plaster house. Nearly everyone was laughing, having a good time.

And there he was in front of me, grinning.

"That was fast," I said.

"Fast?"

"Your answer to my prayer."

"I work in mysterious ways."

"No argument there." I hesitated, unsure how to bring up our last meeting. "Looks like you've put on some weight," I finally said. Then added, "No thanks to me."

"Oh that." He shrugged. "Don't beat yourself up about it. Folks always think it's better to take the fast shortcut than the longer, eternal route. And it's not like it'll be the last time it happens."

"By me?"

"And others."

"You mean . . ." I glanced around, lowering my voice. "Like Judas? You know about him, right?"

He motioned across the crowd to a big-chested man, sipping from a clay cup, obviously enjoying holding court with a couple younger guys. "And Pete, over there."

I turned and stared. "Saint Peter?"

He nodded. "You're in good company. My number one guy is also going to try and talk me out of the mission."

I tried not to gawk.

"In a few months I'm going to have to share a little *tough love* with him."

I quoted, "'Get behind me, Satan?'"

"So, you *have* been doing some reading."

"Isn't that why I'm here? That, and all the other stuff I've been working on?"

"Stuff?"

"Cleaning up my act so we can get back together."

"Ah. So, we're back to religion. I suppose some of that will stick—at least for a while."

"Excuse me?"

"Don't get me wrong, those are all good things, but . . ."

"But?"

"Righteousness by the flesh—well, it's going to die by the flesh."

I frowned.

"But righteousness by the Spirit—now, that's a keeper."

"You lost me."

He smiled. "So, what else is new?"

I caught myself returning it with a half-shrug.

He (and I'm going to call him, Yeshua, with apologies to my religious friends—and probably my non-religious ones, too) glanced about the crowd. He spotted an elderly couple, their faces lit by the flickering flames of a small, oil lamp in each of their hands. The man's eyes were closed, his sun-weathered skin looking like leather. The woman wore a thread-bare shawl over some very hunched shoulders.

"Jacob?" Yeshua called.

The old man did not answer.

"Jacob!"

The woman gave him an elbow to the side. Startled, he opened his eyes. She nodded in our direction.

"Your lamp?" Yeshua called over to him. "May I borrow one of your lamps?"

The man scowled, obviously not liking the idea. His wife had a different take. And, after a sharp word or two, he did her bidding and brought it to us.

"Thanks," Yeshua said.

The man grunted and motioned toward the house. "They ever going to be done?"

Yeshua grinned. "Good things take time."

The old man waved off the comment and shuffled back to his wife.

"What was that about?" I asked.

Ignoring my question, he nodded to the flame. "Your goodness, your righteousness, it's like this light. Good for finding your way in the darkness."

"Okay . . ."

"But what's really burning here, the wick or the oil?"

I stared at the flame. "Well, the oil. I mean the wick draws up the oil, but it's really the oil that's burning."

"Exactly. And if the wick is independent of the oil . . ."

"It'll burn itself out."

He nodded. "The same goes for your righteousness. You may be able to sustain it for a while, but you'll eventually burn out."

"And the oil is—" I took a stab, "let me guess, God?"

"His Spirit, that's right. The trick is to stay saturated with him."

"We're back to relationship."

"Very good."

"So, being righteous on my own, without the oil's power, that doesn't count?"

"Only if you want to be full of pride and judgment."

"Then how did I make it back here, if it wasn't by being extra good?"

"You made it back here by being extra hungry." He paused, then continued, "Blessed are those who hunger and thirst for righteousness."

I felt my frustration growing. "So, everything I've done to get here has been totally useless?"

"Just the religious part."

"I've been 'hungry' as you call it for days. I've been trying to connect with you."

"Of course."

"Of course?"

"I'm the bread of life."

"Come again?"

"Later. We'll get to that later."

I let it go. "So, I've been trying to connect with you and you just, just . . ."

"Disappeared? Stepped away?"

"Well, yes," I said. "But if I say that, you're just going to tell me you've always been here, you never step away, and somehow it's all my fault for—"

"But I did."

I stopped. "Excuse me?"

"I did step away."

"But—"

"Isn't that how you teach children to walk? You step back a little and let them reach out for you?"

"I don't have kids."

"Ah. Well when you do, you'll discover—"

"When I do?"

". . . becoming a father will radically change your understanding of me."

"Wait, are you telling me I'm going to be a father?"

Spotting a passing boy in his late teens, he held out a hand. "Hey, Zach."

The kid looked up and came to a stop.

"You going to finish that?"

The boy looked down at the cup he held, then back up, giving a silly grin. That's when I noticed his red cheeks and watery eyes.

"Probably had enough, don't you think?"

The boy gave another grin then handed the cup over to Yeshua—who then passed it on to me. "Go ahead," he said.

I hesitated.

"Give it a try."

I brought the cup to my lips and took a sip. It was wine. I'm no connoisseur but even with my uneducated palate, I could tell it was good. Very good.

Watching me, he continued. "Did you know the best wine comes from dry, rocky soil?"

"I'm guessing this is another teaching moment?"

He grinned. "If the soil is too rich, the water too easy to come by, the roots don't have to work, they don't have to branch out and reach for the best nutrients. The vine will bear fruit, yes, but it usually winds up watery and taste-less—not rich and flavorful."

He paused, knowing I'd take the bait.

I didn't disappoint. "So, you stepped back to make me grow some roots. You played this game of hide-and-seek to make me go deeper." He started to answer but I wasn't finished. "Okay, fine, but deeper into what?"

He waited until our eyes met. "Not what. Who."

I stared, waiting for more.

"I'm not a flirt, Will. And I'm certainly not some game." He paused, eyes still locked onto mine. "I am life. Joy-filled, peace-filled, abundant—life."

The boldness of his claim set me back. Suddenly, he wasn't the good-natured, humble guy I started to like. Now he was . . . well, I don't know what.

He must have read my discomfort because he motioned back to my cup. "Drink up."

I did. This time taking a hearty swallow.

"What do you think?"

"About the wine?" I said. "It's good. Really good."

"Thanks."

"Thanks?" I frowned. "What do you—" And then it hit me, the pieces coming together. "Wait a minute—is this, uh—" I couldn't think of the name.

"Cana?" he asked.

"Where you turned the water into wine?"

He smiled.

My jaw slacked. "But I just—I just spent the last half hour dumping my wine out—some very expensive bottles."

He broke out laughing. "And I just made 180 gallons."

Before I could respond, we were interrupted by the sound of clapping. I turned to see the door to the house we gathered around opening a crack, its amber light spilling onto the villagers' faces.

"What's going on?" I said.

The door opened wider and the crowd broke into cheers as a young man with a sheet in his hand emerged. He was followed by a young woman wearing a gown of intricately embroidered blues, greens, and purples. On her head, she wore a band of what looked like gold coins.

I motioned toward the couple as they were ushered to a pair of wooden chairs just outside their door. "What's happening?"

Yeshua raised his voice to be heard over the crowd. "They've just had sex."

"*What?*"

Once in the chairs, the couple were raised onto the shoulders of several laughing, jovial men.

"You're celebrating sex?" I said. "The whole town is celebrating them having sex?"

"Of course. It's a big deal." He turned to see the look on my face. "You don't do this?"

"Well, no—not exactly."

The women in the group began singing as he continued looking at me, waiting for more.

I tried to explain. "It's good and everything, nobody denies that, but not like this." He seemed confused. I continued. "For us, today's kids and my friend, Sean, it's more like, it's like having a real good pizza."

"A pizza?"

"Well, yeah, it's this tasty, Italian dish that's—"

"You've reduced sex to having a pizza?"

"Okay, but at least we're not being prudish about it."

"Prudish?" He motioned to the crowd. "You call this 'prudish'?"

By now everyone had joined in the singing and clapping as the couple was carried through the village. "Hail beautiful Queen!" they shouted. "Blessings to you, mighty King!"

But my companion barely noticed, obviously more concerned with our discussion. "What other gifts have you ruined? What other—no, I don't want to know. It'll just depress me and this is a time for celebration." He nodded to the remainder in my cup. "Go ahead, finish it."

I took a final gulp. It was as tasty as the first. "You know," I shouted, "I think you've been getting some bad press."

Before he could answer, an older, more neatly dressed peasant appeared through the crowd. "Please, Rabbi," he said, "come and speak a prayer over the children."

But Yeshua wasn't finished with our conversation. "What do you mean?" he asked me.

"I mean you're not exactly a buzzkill."

"A buzzkill!"

"Please," the older man insisted, "give them your blessing."

Yeshua nodded. "Certainly." Then, back to me he said, "A buzzkill?" He could only shake his head. As the man pulled him into the crowd he turned back to me one final time and shouted, "*Buzzkill!?* We've got to talk!"

CHAPTER
SEVEN

BY THE NEXT morning I had plowed through the Gospels of Matthew, Mark, and most of Luke. Fascinating. Some of it I remembered. Much of it I didn't buy—particularly the miracles, the healings, and those far-fetched accounts of raising people from the dead (so far, I'd counted three). But all the versions seemed to get his personality right—at least according to my imagination or delusions or whatever you want to call them—intelligent, insightful, affable, and no lack of self-esteem.

I was just getting to his parable about the lost sheep when the doorbell rang. I knew better than to expect Amber to answer it. She'd have to be up and it wasn't yet noon. I rose from the desk in my office, tripped over sleeping Siggy, "Atta boy, Sig," headed down the hall, and crossed the living room to the front door.

Opening it, I saw nothing but a two-by-three-foot box with a smiling Amazon logo. Odd. Except for an occasional book or two, I never order anything from them. The delivery label proved my point. It was addressed to Ambrosia

Driscoll. I frowned, then instinctively checked my back pocket to ensure I still had my wallet and credit cards.

"They're fast," Amber's voice startled me from behind. I turned as she scooted past to pick up the package.

"How did you—do you have a card?" I asked.

"Mom's," she said as she pushed past me into the house. "Took a couple tries to find one she hadn't maxed out."

I shut the door and followed her to the kitchen counter where she set the box to open it. She turned it over, then over, looking for something to grab hold of, a lose end to pull. There was nothing. "Stupid box," she muttered. I reached into my pocket and pulled out my keychain with the miniature Swiss Army knife as she tried unsuccessfully to punch holes in the top with her fist shouting, "Seriously?"

"Here," I said.

She took the knife, stabbed a hole in the box and began sawing back and forth. I wanted to point out she'd have better luck cutting along the taped seams, but I figured, like everything else I said, she'd find the suggestion intrusive. I was pleased I'd begun understanding the adolescent mind.

I was not pleased over what she'd ordered.

"Party hats?" I said. "Noise makers?" I picked up a package of balloons and turned to her.

"New Year's Eve," she said. "We talked about it, remember?"

"No, I don't think we—"

"And you said it would be okay to have a party as long as I didn't drink."

"A party?" My anxiety level rose. "Here?"

"Of course, here."

"I don't know the first thing about . . ." I felt the back of my skull tightening. "Who would we invite? I don't have that many—"

"Friends?" she said. "Yeah, I know. Don't worry about it, we're taking care of everything."

"We?"

"Me and some Darlene chick." She tore into the package of noise makers.

My mind raced. "Pratford? Darlene Pratford?"

"She was the first from the school directory to return my e-vite."

"You invited the faculty from my school directory?"

"I invited everyone from your school directory. Teachers, students—"

"Amber!"

"Chill. Darlene told me hardly anyone will come."

"Why'd she say—"

"Cause you're a stuffy old fart no one likes."

I took a moment to regain my footing. "You and Darlene Pratford are going to throw a party?"

Even with her back to me I could hear the eyes roll. "Very good."

"Here?"

"English—it's your first language, right?"

"Amber."

"Ambrosia." She tossed the noise makers on the counter and headed for the hallway. "I'd love to stick around but there's lots to do." She disappeared around the corner.

"Amber? Ambrosia!"

She popped her head back in. "By the way, when are we going clothes shopping?"

"Clothes shopping?"

She nodded then disappeared again, her voice trailing behind. "I'll need something hot for all those college boys."

❧

I headed back down the hallway to my office, already hoping and, yes, I'll admit, even praying for another one of my encounters. Every day my life grew a little messier, my anxiety a bit higher. If my visitations were in any way real and if he could do what he claimed, it was time for him to deliver the goods and actually provide some help.

I'd barely shut my office door before a strong wind blew against my back. I turned and was standing in a storm on a hilltop. It was night. Below me was some sort of sea or lake.

"Hey there," he called from a small outcropping of rock where he sat, the wind tugging at his clothes and hair. Without invitation, I crossed to him, sat down, and cut to the chase. "You've got to stop her."

"Her?"

"This invasion of my space. All my peace and quiet."

"I thought you were bored?"

"She's invited my entire college to a party at my place."

"Sounds like fun."

"Fun? It'll be awful. You don't know these people."

"Maybe I do."

I sighed angrily.

"So, what do you want me to do? What do you need?"

"I don't know."

"Some extra wine?" He turned to me. Even in the dark I saw the twinkle in his eyes.

"That's not funny."

He shrugged.

"All I'm asking is you just fix it, all right? Fix her."

"By . . ."

"I don't know, do one of your miracle things."

"You don't believe in miracles."

"I'm praying. Doesn't prayer count for something? Isn't this a prayer?"

"I suppose." He looked back out over the water. "At least a cheap version of one."

"Cheap version?"

He turned back to me. "Instead of running from the situation to me—how about bringing me into the situation through you?"

I frowned. "Say again?"

He started to answer, then shook his head, thinking better of it. I waited, but he said nothing more. There was only the sound of wind blowing through the grass and whipping at our clothes. I glanced around and saw nobody else. "Where is everybody?" I asked. "What are you doing out here by yourself?"

"I do this whenever I'm under pressure. 'Daddy and Me' time."

I winced at the childish phrase. Then again, maybe it was just remembering my own dad—long story with no happy ending. "What about your disciples?" I asked.

He motioned down to the lake. In the distance, barely visible, a small boat bucked and fought against the storm. Turning back to me, he motioned to the package of balloons I still held in my hand. "What do you have there?"

"Oh, these?" I said. "They're balloons."

He looked puzzled.

"For parties." He still didn't seem to understand so I tore open the pack and handed him a red one. "Check it out."

He took it and turned it over, carefully examining it. He even stretched it a little. "For parties?" he repeated.

"They float," I said. "You bounce them in the air."

He looked skeptical.

"It's true."

To prove his doubts, he opened his hand and let the balloon fall to the ground.

"No, no," I said. "You have to blow it up first." I scooped the balloon from the grass, raised it to my mouth, and blew. As it expanded, the look on his face was priceless. Once it reached full size, about that of a grapefruit, I tied it off and tapped it over to him. The wind caught it and he had to jump to grab it. Holding it in both hands, he gave it a shake, then held it to his ears, then tried looking inside.

I laughed. "It's just my breath. I increased the air pressure inside so it matches the air pressure outside."

He continued to examine it, thinking. "So, this—"

"Balloon," I said.

"So, this balloon was created to hold your breath?"

"Exactly. And without it . . ." I took a yellow, deflated one from the package, tossed it into the air and let it fall. "See, it's all about air pressure."

He nodded. "With your breath it does what it was created to do."

"Exactly."

He continued staring at it.

"You still don't understand?"

"Yes—" he answered slowly, "I do." Then looking back at me he said, "But do you?"

I knew it was one of his trick questions, so I waited, knowing there'd be more. I wasn't wrong.

He pointed to the deflated balloon on the ground. "That, that is—mankind."

"Oh boy," I half teased. "Another metaphor."

He ignored me and motioned to the storm around us. "And all this, this is the world with all of its worries, its concerns, its pressures." He nodded to the inflated balloon still in his hand. "And this is man when he's filled with God's breath."

I watched as he stooped to pick up the yellow balloon. "But this one, it can't function the way it was created until . . ." He looked to me, waiting for the obvious answer.

I was slow, but not that slow. "Until someone breathes into it."

"Until God breathes into you. Yes. Then his Breath, his Spirit, pushes back against life's problems so they don't crush you."

"Equalizing the pressure."

"*Overcoming* the pressure. And the more of His Spirit you allow inside, the more peace you have, the lighter your burden becomes." He tapped the red balloon back to me, but the wind caught it, raising it above our heads, and whisking it down to the beach.

"And the balloon," I asked, "what does it have to do?"

He shook his head. "Nothing."

"Nothing?"

"It just has to allow him to fill it."

I watched the balloon blow onto the lake, skipping across the water and into the darkness. "So—" the pieces were finally coming together, "when you say, 'Take God to the problem, instead of the problem to God . . .'"

"A better prayer is asking him to fill you first, so you two can enter the problem together."

I stared out at the water. "You're pretty good at this."

"So are these." He tossed the deflated balloon back to me. "Too bad I can't use them here."

"I guess you're just stuck with those farming parables."

"When life gives you olives, make olive oil."

"A little first-century humor, I get it." We chuckled and turned back to the lake. "And the boys out there?" I asked. "In the boat?"

"I'd say the outside pressure down there is a bit over-whelming, wouldn't you?"

"But you're not going to let them drown."

"Not on your life." He rose to his feet and started down the hill toward the lake. "Come on," he shouted. "I think you're going to like this."

Suddenly a light came on. "Wait a minute? You're up here watching them in a storm. Is this the part where you walk on the water?"

"Come on," he called.

I scrambled to catch up. "Wait, wait!" I shouted. "Did you really do that? Did you really walk on water?"

"The fellas wrote about it, didn't they?"

"But that's not possible." I half-walked, half-slid down the grassy knoll until I joined him. "You can't break the laws of science."

"Laws?"

"Facts based upon scientific observation."

"Like the angels you didn't see with me when we first met?"

"Right. There's no proof they exist in a three-dimensional world."

"Three?" He broke out laughing. "Who said there's only three?"

"What?"

"Dimensions." He shook his head. "That's so Greek of you."

We reached the beach as pebbles and sand crunched under our feet. But only for a moment. I glanced down to see why they stopped. The answer was simple. We no longer walked on the beach. We had stepped out onto the water.

"Wait!" I cried, coming to a stop. "What are we doing?"

"Breaking the laws of science."

"This is impossible!" The words barely left my mouth before I felt cold water wrapping around my ankles, then my calves, then my knees. "I can't do this!"

"If you say so."

"Wait!" I shouted after him. "Hang on a second . . ."

And then he was gone. So was the wind and lake. I stood alone in my office.

CHAPTER
EIGHT

THE SPECIAL EFFECTS were interesting, I'll give you that. Still, it wasn't anything I hadn't seen in one of those comic book, superhero movies. Was I a hard sell? Am I a 21st Century, educated human? But it was the other thing that stayed in my head and haunted me. The comment about bringing God into my problems, instead of running away from them to him. That whole balloon business of overcoming pressure. Pretty simple. A childish illustration but it wouldn't leave me alone.

Which may explain why Siggy and I barely hit the beach before I was with Yeshua again. I'm guessing it was early morning. He was sleeping against some cushions. My surprised gasp, which seems to accompany these little rendezvouses, must have awakened him.

With eyes still closed, he asked, "Back so soon?"

"Uh, I guess." I glanced around in what appeared to be the back of a small boat. "Sorry to wake you."

"What's up?"

"About last night, or whenever. I've got a question."

He smiled as his eyes fluttered open. "Just one?"

Before I could reply, a kid in his early twenties called from the front of the boat. "Heads up, Rabbi. Looks like we've got company."

I ducked, dropping to the cushions to hide from him, but of course there was no reason. "They still don't see me, do they," I whispered.

Yeshua rubbed his eyes. "Why should they, you're the only one who matters."

"Me?" I motioned to the other men standing not a dozen feet away. "What about them?"

He laughed and slapped me on the knee as he sat up. "We're talking about an infinite God, Will."

"But—"

"Trust me." He rose to his feet, stretching. "It's not a problem."

I stood to join him. In the distance, I heard shouting. We shaded our eyes against the sun and saw, thirty yards ahead on the shore, a man leaping and screaming. Except for the dried mud and caked-on dirt, he was naked.

Keeping his eye on the man, Yeshua said, "But whatever you ask, better make it quick."

I stared as the wild man waved his arms in every direction. The heavy chains clasped to his wrists flew crazily—and dangerously.

"I'm serious, Will. What's on your mind?"

"It's just—" I tried to focus. "You talked about God overcoming outside pressures."

"From inside with his breath."

"Right. We should bring him into our problems, instead of running to him with them."

"Correct."

The boat continued its approach as everyone kept an eye on the screaming man.

"That's what I don't understand."

"If we trust him," he explained, "running away is never an option. It may not make sense at first but if we bring him into the situation and go the distance, the *whole* distance, he always wins. God never plays defense, Will. Never." With that, he started toward the front of the boat but not before repeating, as much to himself as to me, "*Never.*"

The boat scraped against the beach and shuttered to a stop. The one-man greeting party raced at us, stopping only at the water's edge, leaping and shrieking, eyes wild, spit flying. The men up front, took a step or two back but Yeshua moved forward until he reached the bow. The madman stood ten feet away, snarling, waving his arms, the heavy chains flying. Amidst the screams, we began hearing intelligible words. "What have you . . . with us? Son of . . . Most High!"

I may have been the only one who noticed, but Yeshua stiffened slightly.

The madman sneered, "Oh, we know who you are!" He broke into maniacal laughter. "Yeshua, Son of God!"

"Rabbi . . ." Peter, the big man I saw at the wedding, gestured for Yeshua to stand back. If he heard him, he didn't acknowledge. Instead, after a deep breath of resolve, Yeshua stepped off the boat.

Surprised, the madman stumbled backward. But it didn't lessen his threats or his screaming.

Yeshua sloshed through the water and onto the beach.

"Stay back!" the man shouted. "Stay away!"

He continued forward.

The madman staggered back another step, and then another, shouting, "Have you come to torture us!" He waved his arms, the chains barely missing Yeshua who just kept approaching. "No!" the man shrieked. "Not before our time! No!" He began pleading, "No—please—please . . ."

The desperate shouts slowed Yeshua to a stop. He watched as the man seemed to wilt, lowering his arms, looking anywhere but into Yeshua's eyes.

With a face filled more with pity than fear, Yeshua slowly raised a hand.

The man cowered. "Don't torture us! Please, we beg you!"

Quietly, Yeshua asked, "What is your name?"

The man raised a hand to protect his face. "Don't throw us into the Abyss! Please!"

"What is your name?"

In a last attempt of bravado, the man screamed, "My name is Legion!" He looked up, glaring at Yeshua. "For we are many!"

Yeshua held his ground.

The man's gaze faltered. He looked away, then slowly pulled into himself. "Please—please, don't cast us into the Abyss." His voice grew high and wavery. "Please, we beg you . . ."

They stood like that a moment—Yeshua standing, watching. The madman trembling, whimpering. There was no other sound, except for a breeze rippling the boat's sail and on an adjacent bluff, the faint rooting and snorting of a small heard of pigs. Hearing them, Yeshua looked over to the hill.

The madman spotted his gaze. "Yes!" he cried. "Yes, the pigs! Send us into the pigs. Anywhere but the Abyss. The pigs, the pigs!"

Yeshua paused as if giving thought. Then, simply, quietly he spoke a single word. "Go."

The man's body convulsed. He threw back his head and let out an unearthly scream from deep in his gut. Long and loud. As much animal as human. It echoed off the bluff and faded as the man collapsed to his knees, fighting to breathe. But it wasn't over. He screamed again, a shorter burst, and then again, even shorter—until he crumbled to the ground on his side, chest heaving.

Yeshua lowered to his own knees and began stroking the man's crusted hair. The desperate gasps became pitiful sobs. Yeshua moved closer and pulled the naked, mud-caked body into his own.

We watched, speechless.

"Someone give us a hand," Yeshua called.

No one moved.

He tried again. "Pete, grab the extra robe you brought."

The big man hesitated. "Uh—do you . . . it probably won't fit."

Yeshua gave him a look.

"Right." The big man turned and ambled to the back of the boat.

One by one the rest of us cautiously stepped off the vessel and onto the shore. Over on the bluff, there was a commotion. I looked up and saw the pigs running, racing crazily into each other—until, as if by consensus, the entire heard turned and stampeded to the edge of the cliff where they began to jump off, squealing as they fell, splashing into the water with unceremonious grunts and cries.

I approached Yeshua and the madman, nearly gagging from the smell. Apparently, the black and brown smeared on the naked body wasn't just mud. But it seemed to make no difference to either of them as they continued holding one another, both of their faces wet with tears.

Covering my nose and mouth, I knelt to Yeshua and whispered, "That was . . ." I searched for an impossible word.

"Amazing?" he said.

"Well, yes, to say the least."

He glanced up to the rest of the group who were gathering around. "Jude," he said. "Let's get him something to drink, shall we?"

A younger man nodded and headed back to the boat.

Keeping my voice low, I whispered, "Weren't you frightened?"

"Of course, I was frightened. Wouldn't you be?"

"Well, yeah. But—I mean . . ."

"God never plays defense, Will. Never."

CHAPTER
NINE

SEAN SHOUTED OVER the music in my living room, "You gotta loosen up!" He sported his perfunctory bow tie, this time with a mistletoe motif. Because of the relentless pounding from the DJ speakers, I was less hearing Sean than reading his lips—no easy task in the flashing strobes, lasers, and colored lights. "You've been holding that same drink all night!" he yelled.

"What about you?" I shouted.

He raised his bottle of Perrier. "Eleven and a half months!" A couple kids squeezed past on their way to the middle of the room. "Getting my chip next week!"

"That's great!" I yelled.

"What?"

"I said that's good. And see, you're still having fun!"

"That's because I know how!" He motioned to his date, a petite blonde easily ten years his junior. He flashed a grin as more kids bumped and passed through, sweeping him into the crowd of dancers, but not before shouting, "And you, my friend, are clueless!"

Of course, he was wrong. Big time. I was the one throwing the party or at least allowing it. Granted, Darlene Pratford and Amber did most of the work, along with whatever was left of my sister's credit cards. I'd tried calling Terra every day with no luck. And since I was continually lectured on how this type of extravagance was necessary to get kids to come—well, if it presented a problem, I'd straighten the billing out later.

The point is, I decided to suck it up and try Yeshua's suggestion—to step into my fears and trust what little of God I believed in, to do his equalizing pressure thing. The only time I drew the line was in refusing to allow them to rent and install some fancy dance floor. "No, absolutely not," I said—which explains why Cindy's and my faint tracks of indiscretion on our all-white carpet had already disappeared under newer layers of dirt and grime.

I circulated, wiping drink rings off the various tables and giving brief demonstrations on the use of coasters. I also managed to clean up a glob of clam dip in front of the big screen where the jock-types were playing video games. Luckily, the cream-colored dip was almost the color of the carpet. Almost.

"Hey, Dr. Thomas!" I turned to see Brad Simmons, one of my students, passing with his date. He motioned toward the garage. "Missed you over at Karaoke."

"Yeah, I—well, I don't know many of the songs."

He laughed. "Guess Beethoven and Mozart didn't have lyrics back then."

"Actually," I explained, "some of their compositions did have—" my voice disappeared under even louder, gut-clenching music. He smiled and moved off, dissolving into the crowd.

The living room was getting packed. How many students? Sixty? Seventy? Amber said she'd e-vited over 200. Regardless the number, I'm sure I'd be hearing something from old man Carothers, our neighbor, as well as the home-owner's association. I was also sure I better move out of the room while there was still room to move. As I worked my way through all the bouncing gymnastics, I searched for Amber. When I last saw her she was hanging out in the kitchen with some older kid I didn't recognize—six foot, not too ugly (in spite of his weirdly sheered hair) and wearing a sleeveless T-shirt emphasizing his frequent visits to the gym. She spotted my approach and shot me a glare, a warning to stay away. But he was cool and gave me a nod. Seemed a nice enough guy, but there was still the minor issue of him being a guy.

"Hey, Will!"

It was Darlene. I did my best to avoid her all evening. True, I was grateful for all her help and for her gracious offer to take Amber shopping. I was even grateful for the way the two of them immediately hit it off, but . . ."

"You want to dance?"

"What?" I said. "No, I uh, I don't—"

"Come on, it'll be fun." She took the security drink from my hand, passed it to a less-bouncy student, and pulled me to a spot where there was room to move. And boy, could she move—waving her arms above her head, throwing her long, red hair, gyrating provocative body parts. And me? I stood frozen in self-consciousness, the proverbial deer in headlights. I had never danced in my life. Well, except for that one slow dance in 7th grade with Lindi Hillis, but we'll get to that later.

"Come on!" Darlene shouted, throwing in a few extra moves for my benefit—which weren't all that helpful.

I felt all eyes turning to me—surrounding students, watching, waiting, preparing to judge me as the old fool I am.

But Darlene didn't seem to notice. Or care. "You can do it!" she shouted.

I felt my ears burning. "No, really, I uh—"

"There's nothing to it!" She did a little shimmy. "Just let yourself go."

One of the students shouted, "Go!" Then repeated, "Go, Doctor!"

I turned to look at the kid and those around him. Their smiles seemed genuine enough, even encouraging. Not the mocking expressions I expected.

Another one called, "Go, Doctor!" Others joined in, "Go, Doctor! Go, Doctor! Go, Doctor!" I turned to Darlene. Seeing my helplessness, she slowed and simplified her moves. She began to simply sway back and forth, side to side, and motioned for me to do the same.

"Go, Doctor! Go, Doctor!" By now half the room was chanting. "Go, Doctor! Go, Doctor! Go, Doctor!"

Face my fears? I had little choice with so many shouting and cheering me on. I leaned onto my left leg, straightened, then leaned onto my right. Darlene gave me a nod and I continued, left, then right, then left. I still felt like a fool, but I pressed on.

"Go, Doctor! Go, Doctor!"

Next, she began swaying her arms to the left, then the right, the left, the right—all the time holding my eyes, assuring me she could be trusted.

"Go, Doctor! Go, Doctor!"

I followed her lead, swinging my arms, and a smattering of applause rippled through the crowd. How long I did that, swinging my arms, swaying back and forth, I don't know. But gradually, with her encouragement and the students' cheers, it got easier. Was I even close to acceptable? By no means. But apparently, I was good enough for the kids to turn back to their own brand of jumping calisthenics.

Was I having fun? Not exactly. But I was no longer paralyzed. I was no longer being held prisoner in my private little, self-analytical, self-conscious jail cell. To celebrate my freedom, I even threw in a spin just to prove my point.

Darlene laughed and threw in her own. And the beautiful thing was no one seemed to notice or care. It wasn't until she turned her back, moved directly to my front and started rubbing her body up and down mine, that the spell was broken, and I came to my senses. Nevertheless, I was grateful for the freedom and when she turned back to me I mouthed the words, "Thank you."

She nodded and continued dancing, oblivious to my slowing to a stop and then moving off through the crowd. I passed several grinning students, a couple even gave me high fives and knuckle bumps. I did it. I met the impossible pressure and emerged the winner.

As I entered the kitchen, I caught the attention of one of my composition students huddled at the counter, sipping what I hoped was a soda. "Elisha," I shouted. "Have you seen Amber?"

"Who?"

"My little niece?"

"The one with all the makeup?" I nodded and she shook her head. "Sorry." She raised onto her toes to scan the living room. "Last I saw, she was hanging with some guy."

I thanked her and headed to the back kitchen door. I opened it to reveal a couple guys vaping and braving the cold in nothing but T-shirts. "Have you seen my niece?" I asked.

"Sorry, Doc," the oldest in a threadbare goatee, said. "Nobody out here but us."

I nodded, but seeing the cars jammed in the driveway and remembering my own youth, I stepped outside and moved along the vehicles to check inside. Some were so closely packed I had to squeeze to get through. I had no idea how they'd get out but I suppose that wasn't my concern.

The cars up at the mailbox and on road had parked a bit smarter and I was grateful to see none blocked my neighbors' driveways. What a strange conglomeration of vehicles—from Beamers to Beetles. SUVs to monster-tire pickups. One in particular caught my attention. A 1970's VW van, covered from bumper to bumper with fluorescent, hand-painted, hippie flowers. The snarling cougar stenciled on one side seemed a bit incongruent to the love-power message but who was I to judge.

As far as I could tell none of the vehicles were occupied so I headed back down the driveway and re-entered the house. Shaking off the cold and working to keep my concern in check, I crossed through the kitchen and back into the living room, skirting the perimeter of bouncing bodies.

There was still no sign of Amber.

I entered the hallway and approached the closed bathroom door. I knocked and called out, "Amber?"

"Go away!" some guy shouted.

"Sorry," I said, then, on second thought, I asked, "Is Amber in there?"

"Go!" This time it was a girl.

I tried the door, but it was locked.

"A little privacy!" she shouted.

I didn't like the sound of that, but at the moment, I had other worries—quickly rising. I headed past my office and the bedroom. I'd had the good sense to lock both but checked them anyway. Good. Still locked.

That left only . . . my eyes shifted to the laundry room at the end of the hall. I moved to the door and opened it. In the dark, lit only by a pink night light, I saw movement. I reached for the switch and snapped it on. The overhead fluorescent flickered and I saw Amber with the guy I'd seen earlier. They were not making out or even having sex as I feared. Instead, she sat on the washer as he was tying off her arm with a belt, holding a syringe between his teeth.

I went ballistic. Without a word I ran straight at him with everything I had.

"Uncle Will!"

Unfortunately, what I had was pretty anemic to what he was packing. I did manage to slam him into the washer. I even struck the first blow—the side of his head from what I recall. Wherever it was, it was enough to knock the syringe out of his mouth. And to make him angry.

"Uncool, man. So uncool." He had a deep, Rocky-esk voice accompanied by a pronounced lisp. Any other time the combination might have been funny.

I'll confess, I'd never been in a fist fight before. Well, except for that incident back at the 7th grade dance. Seems Lindi Hillis's boyfriend took exception to the way we held each other and he went on the attack to restore her honor—or his. I held my own in that fight, well actually it was more like a slap-fest which the chaperones quickly broke up.

But here, in the laundry room, there were no chaperones, it was just me and Rocky Jr. Fortunately, I'd seen enough movies to know what to do. Unfortunately, he'd seen the same movies and several more. Then there were his, aforementioned, frequent visits to the gym. All this proved adequate in coming to his defense.

And a little more.

I didn't see the fist coming at my left temple, nor the multiple punches to my kidney. But I did remember Amber screaming, "Stop it! Stop it! You're killing him!" I suspected she was no longer yelling at me. I also remember the gleaming white surface of the washing machine rushing toward my face and the sound of breaking cartilage—no pain, I figured that would come later. And not just once. I saw the washer come at me again and then again. "You're killing him!"

If there was a fourth contact, I don't remember.

I do remember waking up to the faces of several students staring down at me. I also recall bits and pieces of the EMS ride to the hospital.

And, for the record, I was absolutely right about the pain. It did come.

PART TWO

CHAPTER
TEN

IT WAS NEW Year's Day. A few hours earlier Darlene drove me home from the hospital where they taped my nose and checked for other injuries.

New Year's Day. When the cops came, reports were filed, and Rocky Jr., who no one saw before or after, had vanished.

New Year's Day. According to Amber, the official date of my sister's homecoming. We still hadn't made contact with her but it didn't matter. It had been an entire week and Amber and I'd had enough. If Terra wasn't at home when we got down there, we'd search the entire city of Seattle until we found her. At least that was my plan. It was hard to tell Amber's since that would involve speaking to me, something she hadn't done since my failed search and rescue attempt. Still, the four grocery bags of clothes (some hers, some Cindy's) waiting at the back door were a sure sign she was ready to leave.

All good things must come to an end. And, thankfully, bad ones, too.

It was a little after noon as we sat in the car listening to the drum, drum, drum of the ferry. Generally, it wasn't a long ride to the mainland. But today it was interminable and executed in total silence. Had it been any warmer, we'd have left the car and strolled to opposite sides of the vessel to gaze out over the water. But there was no way either of us was going to endure the freezing fog and spray for the extra solitude—not when we could enjoy the same privacy by simply sitting there and shutting out each other's existence.

But, like I said, all good things must come to an end . . .

"Hey there" the all-too familiar voice called. I blinked and saw Yeshua and I were being jostled along a dry, dusty road by a crowd of his first-century pals. He motioned to my face. "Looks painful."

I reached up to check my nose. Not that I had to. Hard missing the white tape and gauze stuck in the middle of my face. Or the dull, incessant throb.

"Want some help with that?" he asked.

"'Help'?"

He held up his hands like a surgeon who had just scrubbed, then gave his fingers a wiggle.

"Right," I said, anything but amused. "A little Son of God humor. No thanks."

He shrugged. "Suit yourself." Then, more seriously, he added, "But you've got to remember, Will, the brightest victories hide in the darkest places."

"What?"

"Daniel facing the lions, Moses and the Red Sea, Isaac on the alter. Trust me, that's how things work."

"'God never plays defense,' I get it. If you don't mind, I've taken enough of your advice for a while."

"Or not enough."

I snorted; not so easy with a nose full of cotton. I motioned to the people pushing and shoving us along. "Big crowd today."

He nodded. "Here to see another performance I'm afraid."

"'Performance'?"

His eyes scanned the group. "I'll have to thin them out again."

"With what, some of your crazier teaching?"

"Mm," he agreed.

I couldn't resist quoting, "'Eat my flesh, drink my blood.'"

He turned to me, obviously pleased. "You *have* been doing some reading."

I nodded. "Down time in the waiting room," then added, "most people try to build a following. But you, you're really not so good with public relations, are you?"

"I'm looking for people who are hungry for the truth, not for amusement."

"Then you won't be too thrilled about some of today's churches."

He looked at me, quizzically. I shook my head, saving it for another day.

He motioned to a middle-aged man on our right, slightly stooped, worry etched across his face. "As far as truth, take Jairus, there. His daughter is dying and he's come for my help."

"Jairus?" I said, recalling what I recently read. "The synagogue official you met after crossing the Sea of Galilee?"

"Now you're just showing off."

It was my turn to shrug.

A frown wrinkled his forehead and he slowed to a stop. The crowd followed suit. Turning to them, he searched their faces. "Who touched me?" he asked.

Everyone became quiet.

"Someone touched my clothing. Who was it?"

They glanced to each other, several repeating the question as if they hadn't heard. But he said no more, just stood there, silently waiting.

Jairus, the synagogue official, turned to him. "Rabbi." There was no missing the urgency in his voice. "My daughter, she's—"

Yeshua held out a hand, signaling for him to be patient. And, still looking over the crowd, he continued to wait. Finally, Peter, a few feet from us, pushed his way to Yeshua's side. "Lord," he said, "you've got all these people crowding around and you're asking who touched you?"

Yeshua ignored him and remained waiting.

A stirring began in the crowd. People slowly parted to reveal a hunched woman in a tattered dress and shawl coming forward. She kept her eyes fixed to the ground. When she arrived, she was shaking in fear and sank to her knees. Yeshua kneeled to join her and the people murmured in disapproval. As if that wasn't enough, he reached out and took one of her boney hands into his. A gasp rippled through the crowd.

"Rabbi," someone warned. "She's unclean, you must not touch her."

He paid no attention but waited. Slowly, haltingly, she raised her eyes to meet his. Her brown, weather-creased skin glistened with tears. He nodded to her; an encouragement. She looked back down. Still, he refused to speak.

Finally, in a thin, trembling voice, she answered, "I've—been sick—"

"A bleeder," someone scorned.

"Twelve years," an older woman added. "Such sin, even the doctors can't cure."

If Yeshua heard, he gave no indication. He just kept waiting. She looked back up, her eyes locking onto his. She took an uneven breath, "I thought—I thought if I could touch your clothes . . ." She dropped her gaze again, this time breaking into silent sobs.

We all watched, waiting. He reached out and took her other hand. Now both were in his. Finally, he spoke, barely above a whisper. "And?"

She looked back up, a nervous, tremoring smile on her lips. "It's—stopped. I can feel—it's gone."

The crowd stirred, whispering in surprise.

Yeshua rose and helped her to her feet. Standing and still holding her hands, he replied, "Daughter, your faith has healed you."

She pulled her hands from his to cover her mouth, an attempt to conceal her joy.

He smiled. "Go in peace. Be free from your suffering."

Eyes filling with fresh tears, and with a girlish giggle, she raised her arms to hug him until the crowd's gasp brought her to a stop. She understood and, turning, she searched for someone, anyone to share her joy. But they recoiled, confused, unsure how to respond. Seconds ago, no one would touch her for fear of being contaminated, afraid her sickness would be transferred to them. But now—not only had the teacher touched her, but her sickness was contaminated by his wellness—the flow reversed, his health transferred into her.

Yeshua continued to smile, his own eyes filled with moisture—until a young woman near him opened her arms to provide the embrace the woman so desperately needed to give—and to receive.

It was a warm, heartfelt celebration—but short-lived.

"Jairus!" A young man yelled from the edge of the crowd. He and a companion pushed their way toward us. "It's too late!"

"What?" Jairus shouted.

"Your daughter," he called. "She's—she's dead!"

Once again, the crowd began to murmur.

Jairus could only stand there, staring.

"It's true," the young man said.

Jairus choked out the word, "No!"

"We came as soon as we could."

"No!" Jairus shook his head. "No, no, no . . ."

"There's no need to trouble the Rabbi any longer."

The crowd grew stone-silent as Jairus stared at the ground, trying to comprehend. He turned, lifted his eyes back to Yeshua his expression full of grief, resentment—and a furious, roiling question: *Why!*

Yeshua was clearly moved, but it had no effect upon his response. "Don't be afraid," was all he said.

"Afraid?" Jairus's voice trembled in rage. "My daughter is dead! Dead!" He took a breath. "And you could have saved her! If you wanted, you could have saved my little girl!"

Yeshua nodded, then quietly answered, "Just believe."

Jairus glared at him. He tried to speak, but there was too much anger, he could only shake his head.

Without further words, Yeshua turned and started through the crowd, resuming his journey to the man's house. It took a few steps for me to maneuver through the people and catch up.

"He's pretty upset," I said.

"Wouldn't you be?"

"Of course."

"Aren't you still?"

He had me there. "But you're going to heal her, right? That's what I read."

"God never plays defense. But you, like Jairus here, somehow you think you're the exception. You think you've been forgotten, abandoned—when, believe it or not, your growth is right on schedule."

"My growth? So, this is like what, some grand training program, some cosmic setup?"

He continued walking. "You set yourself up, Will."

"What's that supposed to—"

"But don't worry. Sometimes the best learning comes from the biggest mistakes."

"You're saying back in the laundry room, stepping up and facing the problem like you said; you're telling me that was a mistake?"

"'Those who live by the sword—'"

"'. . . die by the sword,' yeah I get it."

He said no more but continued walking—while I continued to stew.

Moments later, we arrived at the house. The place was the typical, one-story, stone and plaster affair. Neighbors were already gathering—crying, some actually wailing, others beating their breasts. I learned later that making a big production over death was their custom. And if there weren't enough friends and neighbors to join in, others were actually hired to heighten the drama. But it didn't matter. Either way, Yeshua wasn't crazy over what he saw.

"What's happening here?" he shouted. "What's all the noise?"

"Their daughter has died," a mourner cried. "Their only child is dead!" This brought another wave of wailing, louder than before.

"No!" Yeshua shouted over them. "The child isn't dead, she's just sleeping."

The group laughed scornfully.

He ignored them and turned back to the crowd. "Peter," he called. "James, John. I want you to clear these people out of here. I want only you and her parents with me. Nobody else." He turned to Jairus and waited until the man wiped his face and gave a tentative, though confused nod.

The boys went to work.

As we stood there waiting, watching, I said, "You're really going to do this thing, aren't you?"

Keeping an eye on the progress, he said, "It won't be the last time."

"You mean, Lazarus?"

"And the widow's son in the funeral procession."

"I read about that."

"And, of course, yours truly."

"The resurrection?" I said. "You're really going to pull that off?"

"Have you ever known me to lie?" He saw the look of doubt on my face. Replying, he said, "And still you're fussing about your nose."

"Shouldn't I?"

He said nothing.

"Well?"

"The brightest victories hide in the darkest places."

I answered sarcastically, "Which is why Amber hates me more than ever."

"And why you'll be called before the college board."

"I'll be called before the—"

"Spoiler alert. Sorry. Listen, we'll talk more, but if you'll excuse me . . ." He started toward the house which had finally been cleared of all the drama. "Time to mess with your three dimensions."

"Wait," I said, "we're not done here. I still don't—"

"Jairus has waited long enough, don't you think?"

I gave a reluctant nod and he turned to enter the house.

"So are we going to sit here all day or what?" Amber asked.

I blinked. The ferry attendant was impatiently motioning me forward. And if I'd missed the point, the cars behind me started to honk. I gave a wave, turned on the ignition, and headed down the ramp to begin our journey to Seattle—and other parts unknown.

ELEVEN

"TAKE THIS EXIT. It's 145th."

"I know where you live."

"So why are we in this lane?"

"Be patient, we'll get there."

With a vintage Amber sigh, she dragged her pink headphones back over her head. I clicked on the blinker and moved to the exit lane to take us to what I affectionately called, "Hell House"—her place of residence and my childhood home. I hadn't been there since Mom died.

I hated the place so much I even gave my half to my sister—though technically, I didn't give it; I sold it to Terra, who promptly moved in and stopped making payments. Not that I blamed her, being a single mom trying to support a kid—and a habit.

I turned left on 145th and stopped at the light on 15th Avenue where a quintessential homeless man stood with a quintessential sign asking for money. I instinctively hit auto-lock, turned right, and paralleled Jackson Golf Course where we used to go sledding before they put up the fences. Even now, I felt a heaviness in my chest. I took a deep breath, trying to blow it out. No luck.

The street was shaded by trees creating a long, dark corridor. I wondered if some of the larger firs and cedars were there when I was a kid. In place of the cheap homes, vacant lots, and horse trails of my memories, there were duplexes, apartments, even a sport's club. Just four blocks later, we came upon a place I expected to be torn down long ago. Back then it was called, Porchlight Tavern. The location of my first and, until last night, only real fight. I was fourteen . . .

It was payday and Mom had ordered me to come down here to fetch my father. She was in no better shape, which is probably why she sent me, either that or she figured the best way to get him to comply was to shame him in front of his buddies.

Either way, my mission was doomed to fail.

I remember walking the five or six blocks in the cold, evening dusk. I remember taking a deep breath and pulling open the door to a blue smoke-filled dimness—a pool table in front of me, a pinball machine to the left, the bar to the right. And the smell of cigarettes and men who'd put in a hard day's work. I also remembered the music, the organ solo opening to, "Light My Fire," by The Doors. My eyes were still adjusting to the dark when I heard a thick, phlegm-filled voice shout, "Hey, Billy, that your kid?"

Heads turned toward me. A hulking form pushed himself from the bar. He was silhouetted by a blue-lit mirror with rows of different colored bottles.

"What you doin' here?" my father asked.

"Mom said—" I swallowed, fighting to hold my own.

"She okay?" He stepped closer, big and burly and terrifying. Funny, to this day, I know everything about his body, but can never picture his face; just those big white teeth he was so proud of. "She alright? What's wrong?" he asked.

"Nothin'. Just that . . ." My mouth was cotton.

"Talk to me, boy."

I swallowed, then croaked, "She said you better come home or there'll be hell to pay."

The room chuckled. So did he. "She said that, did she?"

No longer trusting my voice, I simply nodded.

"How old is he, Billy?" A women's smoke-cured voice called from the bar.

"Thirteen," he said.

"Fourteen," I corrected, my voice high and thin.

"Thirteen, fourteen," she laughed which grew to a set of wheezing coughs. When finished, she said, "Old enough for a beer, don't you think?"

"Yeah. Good point." I felt his hand on my shoulder. "Joel, get my kid an Oly."

I squirmed from his grasp. "No thanks."

My brief moment of backbone surprised us both "What? Not man enough to share a brewsky with your pa?" There was the grin.

I shook my head, stepping further from his grasp.

"What's your problem?" His grin remained but the humor was fading.

"A real man—" and I don't know what possessed me to say it—my mother's seething contempt, my suppressed rage over the years of bullying our family, what I knew he was doing to my sister—I had no idea, but I said it. "A real man would come home and take care of his family."

The room "Ooo-ed."

Again, his hand found my shoulder. This time I batted it away. That's when he cuffed me—hard enough to make my ear ring but not hard enough to stop me from instinctively returning it with a punch of my own into his gut. It was rock hard. The rest was and is still a blur. I do remember throwing a couple more punches, one at his face, until I was on the ground, and he was being pulled off me. I also remember a smear of blood across those big white pearlies, as "Light My Fire" came to an end with the same organ solo with which it began.

We seldom spoke after that. His drinking grew worse, my love for books stronger. And, although I felt guilty, four years later, when I stood before his casket, I was unable to cry.

Back in the car, I turned left and started up a small hill. Funny, how everything is so much bigger when you're a kid. This very street with its slight incline was a mountain slope I raced down on my bike, wind in my face, roar in my ears, until that one time when an errant pothole threw me over the handlebars, severely fracturing my arm—and giving me even more time to read.

After taking another left, I saw the neighbor's front yard terrace, the one we rolled down so many times we were left dizzy, staggering, and sometimes, after too much Chef Boyardee for dinner, a little nauseous. The houses here had not been torn down and replaced. Not yet. And, though the front lawns had not degenerated into parking lots for broken-down cars, many traded in their lawns for weeds— but neatly mowed weeds since even now the neighborhood seemed to have a sense of pride.

"There's her car." Amber ripped off her headphones as I pulled behind a black, Toyota Solaria with blistering paint. The house in front of us looked no better. I barely stopped before she threw open the door and scrambled out. She was halfway up the broken sidewalk before she turned and yelled, "Aren't you coming?"

"I'm good."

"Seriously?"

"Tell her to come on out and we'll grab something to eat. Maybe head over to Ivar's for some clam chowder."

"You really do hate this place, don't you?"

"I've got some messages to catch up on," I said, reaching for my phone.

She shook her head, then turned and traipsed to the front door. Whether she believed me or not, didn't matter. I was not going inside. For the last week, I suffered and babysat for my sister. She needed no more proof of my love, especially if it meant battling memories I worked so many years to forget.

To prove to myself I wasn't lying, I checked my phone. There were two messages from Darlene, another from Sean, two from a couple neighbors (no doubt angry over last night), and one from Dr. Seneca, chair of our department.

Spoiler alert, Yeshua warned. Well, at least he got *that* right.

I finished listening to the first message by Darlene: "Hey, Will, I hope you're okay. I brought over some lunch but you guys had already left. Call me and let me know you're—"

"Uncle Will!" Amber shouted from the open door. "She's not here."

I rolled down the window. "What do you mean. Her car's right—"

"I know! You need to see this."

"What?

She motioned me inside.

"I told you, I'm not—"

"She's not here. You really, really need to see this!"

I swore softly and shoved the phone into my pocket. Stepping outside, I shouted, "Have you looked everywhere?"

"She's not here."

I headed up the sidewalk. "Did you try the—"

"I've looked everywhere. Hurry!"

"So help me, Amber, if this is one of your—"

"Hurry!" She darted back into the house and I followed. The place smelled like cigarettes and dirty laundry. I'd barely entered the living room before the memories hit. There, four feet in front of me, was where we found my mother unconscious, the first time.

I pushed aside the memory and shouted, "Terra? Terra?"

"I told you she's not here!"

I passed by the kitchen—the counter and sink filled with dishes—and quickly headed down the hallway. If I moved fast enough, I hoped to outrun the demons. "Terra!"

Amber stood pointing into the largest of the two bedrooms. My parents'. The room was a disaster, bed unmade, clothes everywhere. But no sign of my sister.

I turned toward the other room. "Have you tried—"

"Look!" Amber pointed back to the first room. "On the floor."

I turned and saw a half-dozen wrappers, mostly clear, torn open, and tossed on the threadbare carpet.

"Paramedics!" she cried.

"What?"

"Those are for IVs and needles and . . . The paramedics were here!"

I entered and stooped to the floor, carefully lifting one. It looked medical, alright, with writing I didn't fully understand. I glanced back to Amber, her eyes welling with tears.

"We've got to find her," she cried. "They took her and we got to find her!"

CHAPTER
TWELVE

IT TOOK TWO phone calls to find the right hospital. There are only so many ICUs in the area. By the grace of God, if you want to call it that, someone had phoned 911. It may have been Terra, but we had our doubts. Not with heroin.

The bone-weary nurse at the ICU station was not crazy about letting a minor into the ward, particularly with no I.D. to prove she was the daughter. The fact that Terra and I had different last names didn't help. But Amber's drama and my persistence wore the woman down and eventually, a younger nurse appeared and escorted us past the seven, glass-enclosed rooms. We couldn't help stealing looks at each of the patients, some sleeping, others unconscious— all struggling in one way or another to live.

It was good preparation for what greeted us in the eighth room.

"Mom!" Amber raced to her mother's bed.

I was a little slower to join them. I couldn't remember the last time I saw her. Was it with Zoom or in person? All

I knew was the bronzed skin she'd always been so proud of, even if it meant spending money she didn't have at a tanning salon, was gone. What I saw through the tubes and hoses was a pasty, almost wax figurine. And those high cheek bones she always bragged about? They only accentuated her hollow, sunken face. My beautiful, big sister was a macabre cartoon of what she once was.

I looked over to Amber. Instead of the tears I expected, she stared stoically down at her mother. No expression. If I read anything, it might have been a certain contempt. Revulsion. Then again, if I thought I knew anything about Amber, it was I didn't really know anything.

Over the faint chirps of a monitor and the hiss of a ventilator, the nurse explained Terra's heart suffered "infectious endocarditis" along with "serious arrhythmia." They were running more tests but it looked like her kidneys were shutting down as well.

"What's the next step?" I heard myself ask.

The nurse glanced to me then to Amber then back to me. "Now, we just wait."

And wait we did. We camped out in the adjacent waiting room—an older area smelling of floor wax and disinfectant. The flickering florescent in the corner did little for the ambiance. Across the room the TV quietly droned with some newscast we barely heard. Amber moved across from me and escaped into her world of cell phone and headphones.

With school about to start, I spent my time with the Emily Dickinson essays I brought along to grade. Or at least tried to. Unfortunately, my little homecoming unearthed too many ghosts for even Emily to keep buried.

"Rough day, huh."

I turned and saw him sitting in the chair beside me.

"What . . ." I glanced over to see if Amber noticed. She hadn't. Lowering my voice, I asked, "What are you doing here?"

"I had some down time."

Noticing he still wore the robe and sandals from his own era, I said, "You just can't hop back and forth like that."

"Because?"

"Because it goes against the laws of . . ." I slowed to a stop.

"Yes?" he asked, that twinkle back in his eyes.

I changed subjects. "Why here, why now?"

"People tend to hear me better in places like this."

Two large orderlies in white uniforms rounded the corner. As they approached, I stiffened, preparing for what I feared would be an encounter. But Yeshua seemed unconcerned. Instead, he looked at them and said, "Fourth bed down," then added, "I'll be there in a second." They nodded and continued to the ICU door. Then, for my clarification, he repeated, "*Fourth* bed."

"Not the eighth?" I said. "She's going to be okay, then?"

"I can't tell you, Will. You should know that by now."

"Right," I scorned. "That would take away all your fun."

"Actually, it would take away all your learning."

I snorted and looked down at the essay in my hand.

"Does that frustrate you?"

"What do you think? Of course, it frustrates me. You're in charge, you make all this happen, and then you refuse to—"

"Whoa, whoa, whoa. You think I made this happen?"

"It's your universe."

"We made it to share." When I didn't reply, he continued. "I knew it was going to happen, absolutely. But I didn't make it happen. That's a big difference."

I scoffed. "*Free will.* I almost forgot."

"It's our greatest gift. If we didn't give you that, you'd be nothing but programmed robots."

"Might make things easier," I muttered.

He sighed. "Tell me about it." Then, "But would you wish that on your kids?"

"I told you, I don't have—"

"Would you wish that on Ambrosia?"

I glanced over to Amber, still lost in her own world.

He continued, "We built into you the desire for human decency and compassion. You even created laws to enforce those desires." He sighed again. "But it doesn't seem to make much difference."

I tilted back my head and closed my eyes. "I feel like a rat running in an obstacle course—and I don't even know the prize. That's some cosmic maze you've designed, I'll give you that."

"Actually, *you* designed it."

I didn't bother opening my eyes. "More free will."

"I'd give anything if you'd chosen a different way to learn. We warned you. We even—"

"Warned us?"

"You could have taken our word for things without having to ingest all that knowledge of good and evil."

"Ingest all that . . . Wait a minute, are you talking about Genesis, the Tree of the Knowledge of Good and Evil? You don't expect me to believe that myth."

"Okay."

"What do you mean, 'okay'? Is it true or not?"

"You're a lit guy. You know you can tell as much truth in metaphors as you can with historical facts." He shrugged. "It certainly works for me."

"You mean the parables."

He nodded.

"So, the Garden of Eden, was it real or not?"

"I think you're missing the point."

I frowned.

"We're dealing with a much different issue here, Will. The one causing you so much pain."

"Which supposedly you could prevent any time you wanted."

"If you'd open your heart and ask me."

"If I opened my heart and . . ." I stopped, suddenly realizing where we were going. "Oh, I get it now. Here comes the sales pitch. I was wondering when you'd get around to it."

"Sales pitch?"

"Repent from my evil ways, admit I'm a wretched sinner, beg for forgiveness, blah, blah, blah."

"Well, the forgiveness part is important, but—'*blah, blah, blah*'?"

"All of this." I motioned to the room. "My crazy visions, your guest appearances—it's all been for what, to convince me to become a Christian?"

"*Christian*? That's what they're calling you now?"

"Not me, I voted Democrat."

He grew quiet. I stole a glance and saw the disappointment on his face.

"What's the matter, you don't like Democrats?"

"Some of my best friends are Democrats. Republicans and Indies, too. But . . ."

"Oh," I said, "it's the name, Christian."

"I was hoping for something a little more personal. You know, like 'friend.' I'm also pretty fond of, 'brother.'"

"Doesn't matter, I'm out."

"*Out?*"

"No way am I joining your band of narrow-minded hypocrites."

"Good. I've got enough of those already."

I wouldn't let that derail my rant. "Jumping through hoops, saying the magic words, having to—"

"Wait. *Magic words?*"

"Yeah."

"So, I'm like a club? Something you join?"

"Sort of."

"What, with special words and secret handshakes?"

"I don't know about the handshakes. Maybe. The point is, you're either a member or you're not. Either in or out."

He grew silent again, then began to nod. "Binary," he said.

"What?"

He motioned toward Amber's cell phone. "Like your computers."

"You know about computers?"

"I do a little reading."

"Down time," I repeated.

"Binary," he said. "In or out—yes or no. So now I've been reduced to two dimensions." He shook his head. "Those Greeks. Is there anything they haven't messed with?"

I frowned again, having no idea where he was going.

He leaned forward, spoke more intently. "Look, you've read enough about my life by now. How many times, when the boys came to me asking is it this thing or is it that thing, is it yes or no, how many times did I give them the answer they were expecting?"

"I don't—"

"Come on."

"I really don't—"

"Zero."

He waited for my response. When I didn't give one, he continued. "Over and over again, they'd ask me, 'Which is it, A or B? Yes or no?'"

"And your answer?"

"Oranges."

"Oranges?"

"Or whatever. The point is they didn't even know the right questions to ask. I'm about relationship, Will. About hanging out with you! Not yeses and nos. Relationship." He motioned to the paper I was grading. "Mind if I borrow that?"

I handed him the essay. He flipped it over and looked for something to write with. I pulled the pen from my pocket and handed it to him. He started to write, but the pen was still retracted. He tried a second time with equal failure.

"No," I said. "You, uh—" I motioned to the top of the pen. "You have to click it."

He looked at me, confused.

"You know about computers, but you don't know about pens?" I took the pen and clicked it. "There." I handed it back to him. "Now it will write."

He gave it a look, then started to draw. "Instead of yes or no," he said, "instead of in or out, try thinking like this." He drew a small crude chair in the middle of the paper.

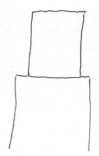

"Let's say this is God. His throne."

"Okay."

"And right here, right next to his throne is this perfect looking guy." He drew a stick figure of a man.

"He's in the club."

"Club Christ," I scorned.

"All right. The point is he plays by all the rules."

"Got it," I said.

"And way over here is another person." He began drawing a figure on the left of the paper. "Way off the grid. Say, a junkie prostitute."

Thinking of something closer, I said, "Or a scum bag pusher trying to hook fourteen-year-old girls."

He nodded as he finished the second figure.

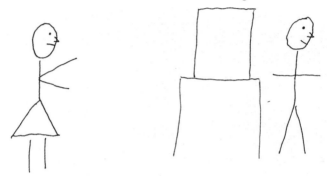

"Now, which of these two would you say is closest to God? The club member or the prostitute?"

"Club member, of course."

"Really? Even though he's looking this way—" He pointed to the face looking away from the throne. "While the prostitute is looking toward God?"

"It doesn't matter," I said.

"Why?

"Because," I searched for the answer. "Because . . ."

"Because he's in the club?" Yeshua motioned to the second figure. "And she's out?"

I stared at the diagram.

"Whose heart is closer?" He asked.

"So—you're telling me . . ."

He waited patiently, letting me connect the pieces.

"But," I argued. "What about getting my act together? All the talk about being a sinner? What about repentance?"

"That's right."

"What?"

"Repent means turning around." He drew an arrow indicating the club member turning his head to the throne.

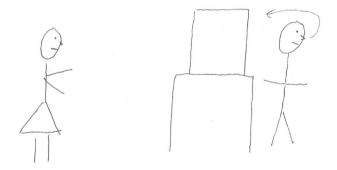

"It means facing another direction—*not* changing who you are."

"But the changing—"

"Is my department."

"She can't keep shooting up and turning tricks."

"Haven't we been through this before? How many of the disciples stopped sinning before they followed me?"

"I don't—"

"How many of them got their act together first?"

"They were all pretty much pieces of work," I admitted. "At least at the beginning."

"Exactly. But the more they lived with me, the more they allowed me to work inside them—"

I finished his thought, ". . . the better they got."

"Until they were behaving as I was behaving, thinking as I was thinking."

"So, I don't have to join the club? I don't have to change?"

"You think too highly of yourself."

"I'm sorry, what?"

"No offense. It's not about you being good or bad, in or out. It's about me."

"You?" I exclaimed. "Being in and out of what?"

"Not what, my friend. Who." He turned and looked at me.

"Me?" I said. "In or out of *me*?"

"It's hard overcoming outside pressure without anything inside."

"You?" I repeated. "You're talking another parable, right? Another metaphor."

He shook his head. "Another fact."

"Now you're going to get all mystical and supernatural on me?"

He looked away, trying not to laugh. "No, Will, I'm not getting all mystical or supernatural." He turned back. "Just higher dimensional."

CHAPTER

THIRTEEN

HEAD TILTED BACK, tepid water pounding my face, the shower was exhilarating. Despite the tub's sluggish drain and standing ankle deep in water, it's exactly what I needed. The tile surrounding me was the same Mom had laid years ago, after Terra tried opening her veins— the second time. We had no money but some stains were impossible to scrub out.

Returning to the house was not easy. But after eighteen hours at the hospital, twice that long without sleep, and going on day four without a shower, well, it became slightly less harrowing. Still, it was Amber who sealed the deal. Initially, she refused to leave her mother's side. But with Terra in a coma, the house twelve minutes away, and the on-duty nurse promising to call the moment there was any change, she finally agreed—*if* I stayed here at the house with her. "And no chickening out by sleeping in the car or going to some stupid motel."

She drove a hard bargain.

I turned off the shower and pulled aside the mildewing curtain, careful not to rip it from any more rings. Stepping over the tub, I dried off with a stale-smelling towel, put on the same clothes I removed to shower, and padded down the hall toward the living room where I'd be sleeping. I refused to look into my parents' bedroom but I did peek in on Amber—who wasn't there.

"Amber?"

I passed the kitchen and entered the living room where I'd thrown a sheet over the sofa and grabbed a blanket for a bed. Still no Amber. I noticed the smell of cigarette smoke and followed it to the garage door leading to the kitchen. It was slightly ajar.

"Amber?" I pushed at the door. It stuck before creaking open. And there she stood in sweats and a flannel shirt, leaning against a pile of boxes, a lit cigarette in hand. She looked up startled, then played it cool, making no effort to hide the cigarette.

Stepping inside, I said, "I didn't know you smoked."

"Found 'em in Mom's drawer." Proving her maturity, she took a drag and blew the smoke over her head.

Suddenly, despite resistance, memories roared in . . .

"That's a crescent wrench, you faggot," he said. "What thirteen-year-old don't know the difference 'tween a crescent wrench and socket wrench?"

I'd swallowed back the shame and crossed to the workbench piled with tools. We'd been working on an old American Rambler—well, I'd been working. Dad sat in a frayed, lawn chair, putting down the beers, and giving me instructions on how to be a real man.

"I swear, sometimes I wonder how you could be my spawn. Like maybe your mom spread her legs to some mental retard when I wasn't around." Chuckling, he added, "Or maybe you're one of them alien mutants, like on the *Twilight Zone*. Sure, why not? My boy, the alien mutant."

We spent all summer working on that car, interior and exterior, until he grew bored, and found some other activity in which to abuse his family.

"Uncle Will? Hey, you okay?"

I blinked and came to. "Yeah, I . . ." Changing subjects, I asked, "Aren't you cold out here?"

"I'm all right."

I nodded. Watching the cloud of smoke still hovering over her head. I tried to resist the obvious but as the designated adult, I had no choice. "You know, smoking . . . probably not so good for the baby."

"She'll get used to it."

"She?"

"Better not be a boy. Unless, of course he's gay, I wouldn't mind that."

The logic surprised me. But it was the first time we'd really discussed her pregnancy, the unspoken elephant in the room, so I took advantage of the opportunity. "Have you, you know, gone in for tests? Done any pre-natal—"

"Done all that crap—vitamins, diet, the whole nine yards."

"So, you're seeing a doctor."

"Nah."

"Then how do—"

"Internet." She took another drag, this time blowing it out in a series of what were supposed to be smoke rings. When she finished, she continued. "Lots of good stuff out there, lots of bad. You just need to know where to look. And, trust me, it's a whole lot cheaper."

I nodded, letting it go for now. "And the baby's father? Is he offering to—"

"I hate the S.O.B."

"Hate?" I said. "That's a pretty strong word."

"'Trust me,' he says. 'I'm using protection,' he says."

"But he does know you're pregnant, right?"

"Probably doesn't remember I exist."

I continued as delicately as possible. "Still, don't you think he deserves to—"

"What about you?"

"Excuse me?"

She took another drag and motioned to the garage and house. "'Hate's a pretty strong word,'" she quoted.

I saw where she was going and tried to side-step it. "Long story."

"Yeah, that's what Mom says. Sounds like he was a real piece of work."

I chose not to answer but she smelled the blood. "Mom says he killed Grandma. Is that true?"

The phrase stopped me. Whether it showed or not, who knows, but it didn't stop her. "If it's true, he should have been locked up and thrown away the key."

"There are different ways of killing," I said. I nodded to the house. "You want a coat?"

"You really hate him, don't you?"

I turned for the door. "I'll get you a coat."

"Don't bother."

If she said anything else, I didn't hear. I stepped back through the door but not into the house. Suddenly, I stood on a knoll overlooking a lake in the middle of the night. There were no other lights. Nothing but a full moon bouncing off the water and stars so vivid you'd swear they were Photoshopped.

"Oh, hi," he said. "It's you."

I spotted him kneeling beside an outcropping of boulders that glowed in the moonlight. He looked slightly disorientated. "Sorry," I said. "Were you, you know . . ."

"Praying?"

I nodded.

He rose stiffly to his feet. "Just finishing up." He brushed the dirt from his robe. "So, how's it going?" Finding a suitable rock, he hopped up on it and motioned for me to join him. "Any word on your sister?"

I shook my head and crossed over to him. "Not yet. But I suspect you know. And I suspect that's *not* why I'm here."

"Why do you say that? By now you know how much I care for you."

"I also know how much you like multi-tasking."

He smiled. "Guilty as charged."

We sat in the stillness. Nothing but the sound of crickets and grass rustling from a slight breeze off the water.

"So," I cleared my throat, "we've been here before."

"Same lake, different location."

"And you were praying for . . ."

He nodded down to the beach where a group of men were stretched out sleeping around the glowing remnants of a campfire.

"Your disciples."

"We found lodging for the women, but the boys, not so fortunate."

"And you're up here praying for them."

He motioned to the silhouette of a man, walking further down the beach. "Mostly him."

I squinted to see but he was too far away. "Who is it?" I asked.

"Judas."

I turned to him. "You were praying for Judas? Why?"

Still watching him, he answered, "Because I love him."

"Right," I scorned. When he didn't answer, I asked, "Even though he's going to betray you? How's that possible when he's going to be responsible for you being tortured to death?"

"I knew that when I chose him."

"You chose him, knowing he'd be your enemy?"

"I don't have enemies."

"Right."

Turning back to me, he said, "He's not my enemy, Will. He's a prisoner of war." He saw my scowl and explained. "Like so many of you, he's all knotted up inside. His heart's battered, his soul crippled. And like so many, he thinks the cure is money. Or power. Or reputation. He thinks those counterfeits are going to set him free."

"And they won't?"

"They're like drinking salt water. The more you drink, the thirstier you become . . . and the more damage it does."

"So, you're praying for some guy the whole world is going to hate."

He looked back down to the beach and softly replied, "Who else does he have?"

I felt myself growing defensive. If this was another lesson, I wasn't in the mood. "Why even bother?" I argued. "The guy's going to hell anyway."

"Are you so sure of that?"

"What? That he's going to hell? He betrayed the Son of God."

He motioned to the campfire. "And so will Peter."

"Right, but for Peter it was a mistake. He knows he screwed up."

"And Judas won't? Why do you think he's going to hang himself?"

"Are you telling me—"

He held up his hand and continued. "The difference is Peter knows me well enough to come back. He knows I'll forgive him."

"And Judas?"

He took a deep breath and sighed wearily. "He's in the club—he's just facing the wrong direction." He turned to me, making sure I understood.

"Alright, fine," I said. "But what does your prayer accomplish? What can you possibly pray for?"

"That he'll know me better. That when the time comes, he'll choose a different path."

"He can do that?"

"Free will—"

". . . is your greatest gift, I know. But you know he'll do it. You said it yourself. You knew when you picked him, it's written in stone."

He nodded, then quietly said, "Even stony hearts can melt."

It was my turn to become silent. And, yes, maybe sulk a bit. He scooted off the rock and motioned me to follow. I joined him and we walked up the grassy hill in the moonlight.

"You know," he said, "there's another reason I pray for Judas. The same reason I tell people to pray for their enemies. It's the only way you can forgive them."

"Why would I want to do that?"

"So he doesn't keep hurting you."

I felt the back of my neck tighten.

He continued. "If you don't forgive him, you become his victim all over again. All that anger, all that rage just keeps bubbling up inside you every time you think about him—over and over again, as painful as the very first time it happened. An endless cycle repeating itself—even after he's dead and gone."

"I'm not letting him off the hook by forgiving him."

"And how's that working for you?"

My jaw tightened but he wouldn't stop.

"Unforgiveness is like setting yourself on fire—and hoping the guilty party chokes on your smoke."

"He has to pay."

"It's not your responsibility."

I threw him an angry look and he replied, "'Vengeance is mine says the Lord.' And trust me, he's much better at that than you."

My voice clotted. "So, what do you suggest?"

"Forgive him."

"I can't!" I blurted. "I won't!"

He answered, with infuriating calm. "And if that's your choice, he will always control you."

"It's not that easy! You don't understand!"

"I don't?"

"It's impossible!"

"I know." He motioned back to the lake. "Like walking on water."

I swiped at my face having no idea where the tears came from. "How?" I croaked. "Even if I wanted—"

"Pray for him."

"I—can't." The tears spilled onto my face. "I . . ."

"It won't change the past and it won't change him. But it will change you."

I stopped at a boulder and leaned against it to catch my breath.

And still he continued. "Praying for him will open closed doors you didn't even know existed."

I tried answering but couldn't.

"It won't happen overnight. But keep praying for him—and you'll begin seeing him through our Father's eyes, loving him with our Father's heart."

I looked up at him through swollen eyes, "And—if I can't?"

"It's never a matter of can't, Will. With God's help, it's only a matter of choice."

FOURTEEN

CHOICE? WHAT A joke. If I had a choice, I would have picked a different father. Or had him hit by a truck. And Mom? Let's just say she didn't always play the part of victim. And while we're at it, I don't recall asking Cindy to run off with her boy toy or inviting Amber to bring her train wreck of a life into mine. And I certainly didn't start up these unscheduled visits with my imaginary friend. Free will? Obviously, a new definition of the term.

My sleep on the sofa was a few degrees short of pitiful as I gradually twisted the sheets into an award-winning piece of macramé—until light blasted into the room.

It was like the explosion back at the cave but I wasn't in the cave. And I wasn't on the sofa. Instead, I lay face down in dirt quickly covering my head with my arms. When I finally had the courage to look up, and believe me it took some courage, I saw the shape of a man carved in light. And he wasn't alone. Two other men stood beside him, older, in long robes, gray hair, and beards. Unlike him, they didn't glow, but his reflective light made them glimmer and shine. They seemed to be in conversation but I was too far away to hear.

I did hear another voice, though. Off to my right. "Lord, it's great that we're here." It was Peter. He was on his knees along with two companions, his voice high and trembling. "If you want—I'll put up three shelters. One for you and one for Moses and one for Elijah!"

I couldn't see the figure of light's face but there was no missing the other two men's expressions—pity, incredulity, and just the slightest trace of amusement. A fog began condensing around them, glowing as brightly as the figure of light. It spread out until it enveloped all of us. So bright and so thick we lost sight of each other.

Then came the voice. Impossible to describe. Like standing next to a giant waterfall. But it didn't just roar around me, it roared inside me—my head, my chest, my stomach—resonating through my entire body. And yet, it was tender and intimate. Terrifying power? Tender intimacy? Like I said, impossible to describe.

"This is my son whom I love," it whispered and roared. *"I'm very pleased with him. Listen to him!"*

So much power, anyone foolish enough to still be standing would have done an immediate face plant. And, though I'm not an official, card-carrying follower, it seemed a good enough idea to repeat the procedure and re-cover my head.

How long I laid like that, I can't say. Living in sheer terror can make seconds feel like hours. All I know is when

I had the courage to finally look again, the cloud, the light, even the two visitors were gone. Now it was just Yeshua standing there. The everyday, normal looking, Yeshua. He was reaching down to Peter, helping the big man up onto some very unsteady legs. "It's okay," he kept saying, "it's all right, don't be afraid." The other two men with Peter, eventually joined him on their own unsteady feet.

The next several minutes were strangely quiet as the men gathered their stuff and prepared to head out. I started to approach Yeshua but he motioned for me to hang back a bit. Which was fine with me. Even though I'd read of the event, the idea of someone you know turning into a glow-in-the-dark, action figure—well, it was a lot to process.

I missed some of the Q and A but I did hear him warn the fellows not to tell anyone what they saw until he was raised from the dead. They nodded, though I'm sure they were more clueless than ever.

We were halfway down the mountain, before Yeshua dropped back to talk with me. "So, what do you think?" he asked.

I was still shaken but tried my best to play it cool. "Impressive," I said.

He chuckled at my obvious failure.

I cleared my throat, trying to think of something more intelligent. "So, this," I motioned to his body, "this is a disguise. You're traveling incognito?"

He grinned. "You're talking about the light?"

I nodded.

"In all you've read about me, did you ever read a physical description?"

"People have been describing and painting you for thousands of years."

"I'm talking about the Bible."

I thought a moment, then shook my head. "Actually, no. Lots of descriptions about what you did, but as far as I recall, nothing about what you looked like."

"I wonder why that is?" He pretended to think, but it was an obvious ruse waiting for me to catch up.

It took a moment, but I did. "No, wait. There is one. In Revelation, where you supposedly took one of your disciples into heaven. He describes what you looked like there."

Yeshua motioned to his body. "And did I look like this?"

"Not in the slightest. In fact—" I slowed, "It was more like what I just saw up on that mountain."

"Hm, I wonder why that is?"

I took the bait. "Because—Is it because up there, that's the real you?"

"*Incognito.*" He grinned. "I like that word."

Even as he spoke, I felt my uneasiness return. All the questioning, all the jabs I'd been throwing at him. Granted, I still wasn't sure what was going on or who he was, but evidence was definitely piling up.

"You okay?" he asked.

"Yeah, I just," I cleared my throat again. "I feel bad about being, you know so, so . . ."

"Snarky?"

"Shouldn't I, uh, be addressing you with more . . ." I couldn't think of the word so opted for, "Reverence?"

"Wouldn't hurt. The angels do that. But remember, we created you different. 'Higher than the angels.' In fact, when I told the guys how to pray, I told them to call God, *Father* or *Dad,* not Your Royal—Whatever."

"Dad," I repeated. "A bit informal, isn't it?"

"Only if you're using it to pull him down to your level. But what if it's you letting him raise you up to his level?" He paused to let the thought sink in before continuing. "The problem with reverence is lots of folks use it as an excuse to keep us at a distance, to avoid telling us what they really think. But you, my friend," he chuckled and slapped me on the shoulder, "you really don't have a problem with that, do you."

Even then, I found myself slightly stiffening at his touch.

Reading my reaction, he laughed. "But hey, we can still be friends, right?"

I hesitated.

"Right?"

"Sure," I croaked a bit feebly. "How can I deny the Son of God?"

He grinned. "Rank does have its privilege."

We continued down the rocky trail, silence once again stealing over the conversation.

"So—" he finally asked. "How are things going?"

"With?"

"The whole forgiveness issue."

"Somehow, I bet you already know."

"Humor me."

We rounded a final grove of cypress trees to see a brown, arid plain stretching below.

I was still trying to construct an answer when he quietly quoted, "*Forgive us our sins as we forgive those who sin against us.*" He turned to me. "Sound familiar?"

"The Lord's Prayer," I answered. "Me and Terra, as kids, when the Pattersons next door dragged us to church, that's what we prayed."

"Uh-oh."

"*Uh-oh?* What does that mean?"

"You tell me."

It was another quiz and to be honest, I wasn't in the mood.

"Come on, play with me here. When you said that phrase, what were you actually saying?"

Seeing no way out, I paraphrased, "Forgive me what I've done wrong—just as I forgive others."

He remained quiet.

"Wait a minute." I turned to him. "Are you saying God will only forgive me as I forgive others?"

"Is that what you prayed?"

I clenched my jaw.

"I'm sorry, what was that?"

I answered curtly. "If that's his requirement then I'm out. I already told you, after what he did to my sister, to our family, I can't."

"Can't or won't?"

"What's the difference?"

"The Holy Spirit is responsible for overcoming your can'ts. You're responsible for the won'ts."

"I don't want to! Can't you understand that? You say pray for him. I can't even do that! The words won't come!"

He let a good minute pass before he spoke again. This time on an entirely different subject. Or so I thought. "Did the boys ever write down what I did with the two loaves of bread and the five fish?"

"How you fed 5,000 people?"

He nodded. "With twelve baskets left over. Pretty cool. You should have been there. It was a big hit."

"I bet."

"And what did the disciples give me?"

"You just said it, five loaves and two fish. Another one of your famous miracles."

"And there you have it."

"Have what? What do you mean?"

"Come on, college professor, go deeper."

I looked at him.

"Allegory," he said. "Metaphor, application."

"Another parable?"

He waved me off. "Everything's a parable. Break it down."

I sighed, but he continued to wait, making it clear I had no choice. "Okay," I said. "The crowd needed to eat and the disciples had nothing except five loaves and two fish."

"They gave me all they had and . . ."

"I don't know, you did the rest."

"Exactly. So, the lesson is . . ."

I waited.

"Allegory, metaphor, application . . ."

"If people give you all they have . . ."

"Even if it's two puny fish."

". . . you'll do the rest."

"And personal application?"

I took another breath.

"Come on. Personal application?"

I closed my eyes and said the obvious. "If I do all I can—you'll do the rest." I turned to him.

He was grinning again. "You're getting a lot better at this."

I shook my head, scoffing.

He elaborated. "Getting a grip on forgiveness or anything else you lack is a Father/son project."

I scowled.

"That's the whole point, Will. For the two of you to hang out and do it together. You do what you can and then let him do the rest."

I remained silent.

"Remember the wedding where I turned the water into wine?"

"Of course, 180 gallons."

"I didn't shout or recite some magic incantation. I just told the servants to get the water, to give me what they had. And as they obeyed me . . ."

". . . you turned it into wine."

"They did what they could with what they had. I did the rest."

"But—how do I know the difference?"

"Difference?"

"How far am I supposed to go before I give up and let you take over?"

He shook his head, chuckling. "You're always looking for formulas. But in a relationship, there are no formulas. It always comes down to listening and abiding."

I sighed wearily. "Formulas are a lot easier."

"Which is why religion is so popular; predicting God's behavior, trying to manipulate him—instead of enjoying a living, vital, Father/son relationship."

I shook my head. "You always make things so complex."

"Complex? *Complex?* It's so simple a child can do it."

"Right. Well I'm no child."

"But you are, Will. You're his favorite child."

I gave him a look. "Just like everyone else," I said.

"Of course. When you're infinite, you can get away with that."

CHAPTER
FIFTEEN

"UNCLE WILL! WAKE up, wake up!"

It took a moment to open my eyes. Longer to get my bearings.

"The hospital called!" Amber wasn't screaming, but close to it.

"What . . ."

"We've got to get down there. The hospital called!"

"Right, right." I threw my feet over the side of the sofa and fumbled for my glasses, only to discover I still wore them. Same with my shoes.

She stood at the front door. "Hurry!"

"Right. Just let me hit the bathroom and I'll—"

"Now! We got to go now!"

Twenty minutes later we were racing through the predawn stillness of the lobby— passing with a trace of reluctance, the coffee vending machine. We entered the ICU and were greeted by a mop-top doctor, chart in hand. His creaky voice indicated he hadn't quite passed puberty.

"Um, hi there, Mr. . . ."

"Thomas," I said. "Will Thomas."

He looked down to Amber. "And you must be—"

"You said she had an episode." Her abruptness forced him to retreat to the safety of his chart.

"Um, actually two. We resuscitated once at 3:42 and another at 4:30." He looked up. We waited. He threw a helpless look to the desk nurse. She saw I spotted it and busied herself with paperwork. Left with no alternative, he coughed. "So, uh—if you'd follow me please."

We started past the row of glass cubicles.

"It's almost six," I said. "Why didn't you contact us sooner?"

"Actually," he cleared his throat. "We didn't figure she'd—that is to say—

"You thought she'd die," Amber said.

He cleared his throat again as we continued walking until we arrived at Cubicle Eight. Terra looked no different than the night before.

"What's the prognosis?" I said.

He returned to his chart. "Severe pulmonary edema has already affected her—"

"Severe what?" Amber asked. Instead of looking at him or her mother, she stared at the wall across the room, seeming to brace herself for the worst.

He saw her response. Compassion filled his eyes. He did not return to the chart but spoke directly to her. "Because her heart can't pump blood very well, it's backing up into her veins. As pressure builds, the fluid enters the alveoli, the air spaces in her lungs, which is making it hard to—"

Still speaking to the wall, Amber interrupted, "She's going to die."

He paused, then added more softly, "Her kidneys are already failing."

Silence filled the room—except for the noise of machines.

"So—" I said. "What's next?"

He returned to his chart. "We can continue various heroic measures but—" Another pause.

"But what?" I demanded.

"We'd just prolong the inevitable."

It took a moment but when I trusted my voice I said, "You can't be certain of that."

"I'm sorry."

Amber shifted her gaze from the wall to the floor—anywhere but to her mother. I felt the tightness, a familiar heaviness pressing on my chest. How could it be that simple? One statement by some man-boy and her life was over? One opinion and she was sentenced to death?

"No," I heard myself say. "No."

"I understand how you feel."

"You're a kid. You understand nothing."

"I understand that—"

"Stop it. Stop talking." It was getting hard to breathe.

"If you want a second opinion, I can—"

"I don't want a second opinion; I want her to live."

He swallowed, his Adam's apple bobbing.

"That's what we pay you people for, isn't it? Isn't it!" He said nothing as I struggled to catch my breath. "So do your job. Do your job and keep her alive!"

"I under—"

"Stop saying that! Just—Stop . . ." I leaned over, trying to breathe.

"Here, let me—"

I pulled away from him.

"Uncle Will?"

I turned to her, trying to get enough air. What was happening? I was there to help her. She was the one losing her mother.

"Sir, are you okay?"

"Yeah," I said, gulping a breath. "Sorry, I don't . . ."

"You better sit down."

"Just a little out of . . ."

"Let's get you to the waiting room."

We turned and moved past the cubicles and out into the ICU lobby. What was wrong with me? Yes, Terra was my sister and, yes, she was part of my past—but that was my *past*, something I left behind years ago. And her dying? I'd always known with the drugs it was a possibility. So why this?

Once we settled in the lobby, my breathing returned to normal.

"Just a little panic attack," Mop-Top assured us. "Would you like some Xanax?"

"No, I'm fine."

"I can make you out a prescription if you'd—"

"I said, I'm fine."

"All right. Regarding your sister, if you'd like a second opinion, I can—"

"I do."

"Certainly. No problem." He prepared to leave but not before asking for one more annoying time, "Are you certain you're—"

"I'm all right."

He nodded. "Okay, then. I'll swing by in a few minutes to see how you're doing."

"Fine. Whatever."

He got the message and turned to slouch off down the hallway.

Of course I'm all right, I told myself. It's the lack of sleep. My overnight stay in Hell House. An entire week with an unwanted house guest—all topped off by hallucinations with the Savior of the World. Okay, maybe I wasn't so all right. Apparently being dragged from my safe harbor into a wild, stormy sea without map, rudder, or compass has its consequences. But I'd survive. It was our way.

"Here you go, Uncle Will." I turned to see Amber offering me a cup of coffee from the vending machine. "How are you?"

I closed my eyes at the never-ending topic. Re-opening them, I turned to her. "How are *you*?"

She shrugged. "We all knew it was going to happen sometime."

I stared at her, unsure what to say.

She gave another shrug, then slipped on her pink headphones and returned to her music.

"Amber?"

She turned up the volume.

"Amber?"

No response. Just those little thumbs with peeling nail polish flying over those little keys. I'm not a fast study but if I learned one thing over the past week it was, she needed her space.

And maybe I learned something else, as well. If what I'd been experiencing, if my visitations had any purpose at all, maybe they were to build upon some microscopic remnant of faith. Preparing me for this moment. And if what I experienced had the slightest whiff of truth . . . I looked over to the closed ICU door. Hadn't he said, more than once, it was all about relationship? About being friends? If that was true and if he really pulled off some of those miracles and healings—sometimes with total strangers, let alone praying for his enemies—what should his *friends* expect? If he actually was the person he claimed to be with the power he claimed to have . . .

I hesitated, then turned to Amber. "Hey." She was too deep in cell phone land to notice. "Hey." I reached for her headphones and gently pulled them off. She tried to grab them but was too late.

"What are you—"

"Just—"

She tried reaching for them but I held them back.

"What are you doing?"

"Just give me a second."

"What are—"

"Give me a second!" The sharpness in my voice stopped her. When I had her attention I said, "I think we should pray."

"What? Jesus," she swore.

I almost smiled. "Not a bad place to start."

"You're serious?"

"We've tried everything else."

She looked at me another moment then shrugged. "Sure, alright."

"Alright?"

"Sure. Mom tried it and it never worked, but sure, why not."

I nodded. "Why not."

I wasn't sure how to begin. More than a little self-conscious, I reached for her hand. She hesitated, then let me take it. I closed my eyes and bowed my head. I didn't have the courage to see if she followed suit.

"Dear . . ." I cleared my throat and tried again. "Dear God—please heal Terra, she's my sister—who is also Amber's mother." (It never hurts to be clear.) I wasn't sure what more to add. But it didn't feel long enough to be serious, so I repeated, and embellished a bit. "Please heal her heart, whatever is wrong with it, and whatever else may be wrong with her."

I paused. Not that I expected Amber to weigh in, I just thought, well, like I said, it felt a little short to do the trick. But I couldn't think of any more filler, so I finished up. "In your name we pray, Amen." I waited, trying to feel something, to treat the moment as some holy encounter. When nothing happened, I raised my head and opened my eyes.

"Are we done?" Amber asked.

"Yes," I said, speaking softly so not to disturb any religious vibe. "Yes, we are done."

She withdrew her hand and slipped on the headphones.

I glanced to the seat on my other side. Another guest appearance would have been nice. But apparently it wasn't in the cards. Then again, maybe I didn't need it. Maybe I'd learned enough, maybe I saw enough to actually believe. I settled back into the chair, trying through sheer will to increase my faith—when I spotted the two orderlies Yeshua spoke to the day before. Somehow, they'd made it past me and had reached the ICU door.

"No!" I was out of my seat in a shot. I raced toward them, throwing a look back to Amber. If she saw, she gave no clue. When I turned back to the orderlies they were gone. "NO!" I shouted.

I arrived at the door and threw it open. The ICU nurse looked up from her station, startled. "Mr. Thomas."

I looked to the row of glass cubicles just as the orderlies entered number eight.

"No!"

"Mr. Thomas!"

I sprinted past the rooms, my heart pounding in my ears. When I arrived, no one was there, just Terra and her machines. I'd barely stepped into the room when the rhythmic beeping gave way to a shrill, steady alarm.

"No!" I raced to her. "Stop it! Stop!"

She lay, unmoving.

"Mr. Thomas!" The nurse called from somewhere behind me.

"C'mon!" I shouted, looking around the room. "You said we were friends!"

"Mr. Thomas." She gripped my arm. I broke free.

"You can fix this!" I shouted. "I've seen you! You've got the power. C'mon!"

I heard commotion behind me. Paid no attention. I searched Terra's face for any movement. "C'mon!" I shouted. "We're friends! You said it yourself. Friends don't do this to friends!"

Other hands grabbed me. Stronger. On both arms. They began pulling. I struggled, but they held tight.

"C'mon!"

Another machine was rolled in, Mop-Top right behind. He threw back her thin sheet and ripped aside her gown, exposing bare breasts. Another man appeared, squirting goop on her chest, as paddles with black, coiled cable appeared.

"Give me 300," Mop-Top ordered.

"The machine whined, building power as he placed the paddles on her paper white skin.

"300," someone called.

"Clear!" he shouted.

Click. Her body jolted. All eyes turned to a monitor. The alarm continued.

"Again!"

The machine whined, the paddles placed.

"Clear!"

Another *click*, another jolt.

"C'mon!" I yelled. "C'mon!"

"Get him out of here!" the doctor shouted.

The grip on my arms tightened as I was pulled away. I dug in my feet. "We're friends!" I shouted. "You can do this! I know you can!"

I was dragged past the glass cubicles, twisting and fighting. Amber stood at the nurse's station horrified. "Uncle Will!" But I barely heard over my own gasps and hammering heart.

"Pray!" I shouted to her. "Pray to Jesus, he can fix this! Pray!"

She stared, mouth ajar, as they hauled me past. I twisted my head, looking down the hall. They were still working on her. The walls grew white, then the ceiling and floor, like an overexposed photograph.

"Let's go, pal," one of my handlers said, his voice barely discernable over the thundering in my ears. "Come along and . . ." His words faded. I turned. His mouth moved but there was no sound as his face grew white. Everything white. A chair floated before me. White and far away. Everything white, far away, and whiter—until there was nothing at all.

CHAPTER
SIXTEEN

WELL, ALMOST NOTHING. Within the silence I heard gentle weeping and the shuffle of feet on sand and stone. The smell of hospital antiseptic gave way to arid smell of dust and heat. I opened my eyes, this time to blinding sunshine—and the silhouette of a small crowd walking past. Yeshua led the way, his head bent down.

I raced to join him and demanded, "Why? You could have done something!"

He continued walking, his voice a raspy whisper. "I know."

"You said we were friends."

I waited for a defense, some type of rebuttal. There was nothing. He wouldn't even look at me—he just wiped his face and gave a hoarse, "You don't—understand."

"I don't understand? Try me!"

After another step or two, he whispered, "Timing."

"Timing?" I shouted. "She's dead!" Finally, he raised his head and looked me in the face—his eyes red and puffy from tears. "She's dead," I repeated, "and you could have done something!"

He nodded, then looked away.

"But you refused! And now—" I fought to keep my voice even. "And now *you're* crying? Why? Because you were wrong? Because you made a mistake?"

"Lord—Lord!"

I turned to see a woman running up a small hill toward us. Like the other women, she was heavily robed and wore a shawl over her head. She wasn't pretty but the weathered face and strong jaw gave her a certain handsomeness. Like Yeshua, she was also crying.

He slowed to a stop as she arrived. After the slightest bow she spoke. Not exactly a rebuke, but close. "If you'd have been here my brother . . ." Her voice caught, and she struggled to finish. "If you had come when we asked, Lazarus would still be alive."

Immediately, I recalled the scene.

She continued, "But I know, even now if you want, God will give you whatever you ask."

He reached out and took her hands. The crowd stirred at what must have been forbidden familiarity. But he paid no attention. Instead, he looked into her eyes and earnestly whispered, "Your brother will rise again."

"I know." She swallowed back her emotion but refused to look away. "On the last day during the resurrection."

Still holding her hands, he wiped his face with his sleeve and replied, "*I* am the resurrection—and the life.

Anyone who believes in me will live, even if they die." She started to interrupt, but he wasn't finished. "And whoever lives by believing in me will never die."

Her gaze faltered then dropped.

"Do you believe this?" he asked.

She looked back to him, her eyes brimming with fresh tears. "Yes, Lord. I believe you are the Messiah. I believe you are the Son of God who was promised to the world."

"Martha!" a distant voice cried.

We turned to see another woman, younger, racing up the hill toward us. Behind her, a small group of nearly a dozen people followed.

"Mary!" the first woman called down to her. "He's here! The teacher is here!"

Mary picked up her pace, nearly stumbling as she arrived. Breathless and also in tears, she dropped to her knees at Yeshua's feet. Moved with compassion, he knelt to join her.

"Lord," she sobbed, "If you had been here our brother would not have died." Another accusation, identical to Martha's—identical to mine.

And once again, he seemed to have no defense. Just compassion and tears. It made no sense. If he really had the power, why had he refused to come and help? Why, with his close friends? And why, if it was his choice, was he so emotionally wrecked about it?

At last he spoke, his voice thick with emotion. "Where have you buried him? Show me."

Mary nodded and, with Yeshua's help, rose to her feet. "Come," she said and turned heading toward a small bluff, fifty yards away. I had my own burning questions, not the least being why I was here and why now. But I went along and followed the crowd. We slowed to a stop about a stone's throw from the bluff. Martha, motioned to a large boulder, six feet in diameter, flat and round, resting against the bluff.

Yeshua looked at it a moment then quietly ordered, "Take it away."

"I'm sorry," Mary asked, "what?"

"Move the stone," he said.

The sisters traded looks. "But, Lord," Martha said, "he's been dead four days. You know how he's going to . . ." She lowered her voice to a whisper, "What about the smell?"

He answered, "Didn't I tell you if you believed, you would see the glory of God?"

She started to protest until her sister touched her arm. She stopped, hesitated, then turned to a couple men in the group. "You heard him. Do what he says."

The men glanced with concern to one another. She scowled and motioned them forward. Reluctantly, they obeyed. Once they arrived, they turned to her a final time, confirming her wishes. She nodded. With resolve, they took positions on one side of the boulder and began pushing. But it was too heavy.

"Isaac," the biggest of the two called, "Josiah, give us a hand."

Two younger men, nearly boys, moved through the crowd and joined them. Together they pushed. As the rock began moving, Yeshua raised his face to the sky and said, "Father, thank you for hearing me. I know you always hear me. I'm saying this for the ones standing here so they'll believe you sent me."

The crowd turned their eyes back to the tomb, some already covering their noses and mouths anticipating the stench. But as the rock continued forward, no one looked away. When it rolled far enough for someone to enter, the men stepped back and rejoined the crowd.

They waited for Yeshua but he did not step forward. Instead, he remained standing and simply shouted, "Lazarus! His voice echoed against the bluff and surrounding hills. "Come out!"

No one spoke. I doubt they breathed.

Nothing happened. The people turned back to Yeshua. But he seemed unconcerned, his eyes closed.

As we waited, my mind kept racing. Why here? Why now? Then realization dawned. If this was like the other times, if this was to teach me something—then the answer could not be clearer. He was showing me proof of what he could do with Terra *if*, like the sisters, I would only believe.

The crowd stirred. Inside the cave's darkness there was movement. Then a flicker of white cloth in sunlight— until a body, wrapped like a mummy, slowly emerged. The crowd gasped, several cried out in alarm.

Yeshua turned back to the men who pushed the stone away and said, "Take off his grave clothes. Free him."

They hesitated, looked to each other for courage, then moved into action. The crowd responded, talking, crying out in excitement, as the two sisters stood, hands clasped over their mouths in disbelief. But not me. I did believe. And, emboldened, I pressed through the people to join Yeshua.

"I understand." I grinned, nearly laughing. "I get it. You're showing me this because you're going to do the same thing with Terra."

But when he turned to me there was no joy in his eyes. None of the sparkle. Instead, it was the same grief and sadness I witnessed earlier. And then he spoke. One word and it broke my heart. One word and it destroyed all that we'd been through.

"No," he said.

It was as if someone punched me in the gut. "What?" I demanded. "With all you've shown me?"

He shook his head.

"With all I've been through?"

His eyes again filled with moisture. But his voice remained firm—thick and husky, but firm. "No."

PART THREE

CHAPTER
SEVENTEEN

I'LL SAVE YOU all the boring details about the funeral arrangements. I did it for my dad, I did it for Mom, and I did it for Terra—same funeral home, same cemetery, same everything. They should offer group discounts. A handful of Terra's friends showed up at the memorial service—"Guess they were expecting free eats," Amber muttered—but just the two of us were there at the graveside.

If you expected something like this to draw us closer, you couldn't be more wrong. In fact, it did just the opposite. If Amber was suffering, she never let me see it. If she needed comfort, she never allowed me to offer it. Not that I didn't try. But the more I pushed, the farther she retreated. More of the mysterious enigma called Amber—or adolescence—or womanhood—or, as I mostly suspected, the joys of sharing our family's DNA.

And my so-called rendezvouses? I was through with them as well. My choice. Was I being petulant? Pouting for not getting my way? Hardly. Even if the dreams and visions were real, even if he was somebody special, and even if I was somehow able to connect with him—the fact of the matter is he was not someone I wanted to know. Miracle-worker, maybe—egotistical claims of being God the Son, definitely. But it was his continual insistence upon having a relationship and being my friend, my *intimate* friend, that brought me to calling it quits.

Friends don't treat friends like he treated me. Particularly friends with supposed power. Particularly when you're desperate for them to use that power and when it would take so little effort on their part. I was through with it. If that's his idea of friendship, I was done. Check please.

Not that he didn't try. On three separate occasions, he attempted to draw me back in. But I would have none of it. If he was such an advocate of free will, then I'd hold him to it. By sheer will I was able to put an end to our little meetings—at least during my waking hours. And when I was asleep? Well it's a little harder to control the subconscious.

༄

"Teacher," a voice called from somewhere in the darkness. At first, I thought, I hoped, I was dreaming, that I was back in my classroom. School was about to start up after the holidays and with any luck things would be returning to normal. But the voice was old, creaky, and unlike any of my students. So much for luck. "What exactly does God require us to do?" it asked. "What sort of works does he expect?"

It came the night following Terra's death—my second sleepover in Hell House and I was miles beyond exhaustion. I'd barely hit the sofa before I was standing near a donkey who walked in a small circle. He was yoked to a crude, round rock, a miller's stone grinding wheat thrown on the packed ground before him. As usual, Yeshua was busy holding court, this time with a large group of men. I stood near the back, doing my best to stay out of sight.

He answered, "This is the work God requires of you—" They leaned in, waiting for another great pearl of wisdom. "Believe in me." That was all he said. No surprise there. I'd heard one version or another of that half a dozen times.

They waited but got nothing more, other than the sound of grinding stone crushing wheat.

A young, studious looking kid spoke up. "What sort of sign will you give us so we *can* believe?"

Yeshua turned to him and said, "Sign?"

"Yes. What will you do?"

Yeshua cocked his head at him quizzically. "Healing the sick, raising people from the dead, drawing them back to God—that's not enough?"

An old fellow with tufts of gray, fly-away hair, replied, "Our ancestors ate manna in the wilderness. As the Scriptures say, 'He gave them bread from heaven to eat.'"

Yeshua nodded. "That's truer than you know. But listen very carefully. It wasn't Moses who gave you the bread from heaven. It's my Father who gives you the real bread from heaven. It's his bread that comes from heaven and gives you life."

The men waited for an explanation but got none. Instead, Yeshua stooped to a handful of wheat not yet in the threshing area. Lifting it, he quietly mused, "Unless a grain of wheat falls to the ground it will not bear fruit." He stared at the kernels another moment before tossing them into the path of the mill stone where they were crushed.

"Sir," the older fellow said, "give us this bread so we can always eat it."

Yeshua looked up at him then slowly rose and said, "*I* am the bread of life." He looked over the gathering until his eyes locked onto mine. "Whoever comes to me will never go hungry. Whoever believes in me will never be thirsty."

I glanced away, tried to jolt myself awake. The first time failed, the second time did the trick. I opened my eyes and was back in the real world.

Did I get the metaphor? Of course. Was I still hungry? What honest, thinking person wouldn't admit some part of them is starved to connect with the great, indefinable cosmos. But I'd wasted too much time indulging in these fanciful excursions. And if by some strange quirk they were true, then all my encounters really proved was that he was a liar. "I am the resurrection?" Please. "I am the Bread of Life?" "I am the way, the truth and the life?" Sorry, no sale. I'll find another, more dependable route.

I said he tried three times to reach me. The second was during one of my multiple visits to Terra's bank. Apparently,

I didn't have to worry about the estate. Since she didn't leave a will and since she'd second mortgaged the house behind my back, the V.P. assured me they would be taking care of all those "bothersome details." He'd barely stepped out of his cubicle of an office to retrieve the stack of those details when I heard the bellowing of a bull. I turned to see I was sitting beside Yeshua on a small wall just outside the white building I'd been to so many days, so many lifetimes, before. It was hot, sweltering, and with a dozen irritating flies constantly buzzing. None of this helped my disposition.

He didn't say a word. No greeting which was fine with me. Instead, he stared ahead, intensely watching a dozen men, I guessed to be priests by their elaborate costumes, struggling with a bull about ten yards from us. They had tied a noose to one of its hind legs and were unsuccessfully trying to tie it to the other.

"So—" without taking his eyes from the scene, he said, "Are you done sulking yet?"

I didn't trust my anger and chose not to give an answer. He had the good sense not to press for one. We continued to watch in silence. Any other time it would have almost been comical to see these fancy dressed men scurrying around and fighting a bull as it bellowed and threw its head from side to side trying to gore them. Not today.

I was no fan of the heat or swarming flies and finally said the obvious. "I don't want to be here."

Without turning to me, he answered. "Neither do I."

"So—let me go back. We're through here."

Still watching the spectacle, he sighed heavily.

"You're not letting me go back?" I said. He didn't respond so I let out a sigh of my own with some added sarcasm. "So much for free will."

Still watching the proceedings, he said. "There's a deeper love at work." I shot him a look and he continued, "Sometimes a parent needs to serve their children vegetables, whether they understand it or not."

The priests finally secured the second leg and tightened the rope, causing the animal to bellow as it lost its balance and fell heavily to the ground. The men swarmed over it like ants as it fought and kicked and cried. Within seconds they managed to safely tie the front two legs, although it did land one, well-placed hoof directly into a priest's gut, causing him to stumble backward and fall to his knees.

Serves him right, I thought.

The bull continued to thrash and bellow as two of the men grabbed its horns from behind and pulled back the head to bare its neck. The apparent leader of the group, dressed completely in white, produced a curved, ceremonial knife from the belt of his robe and knelt beside it.

"No way," I said. "Is he serious?"

The animal bucked and writhed while the leader put his knee against its neck, lowered the blade, and slit its throat. Blood spurted from the wound, spraying over the leader's white garment, some even hitting his face. We were too far away to be hit, but close enough to catch the copper smell of its blood, and the odor of urine and feces as the animal lost control of its faculties.

"This is barbaric!" I said.

Yeshua nodded silently. "It's the Father's will."

The blood flowed from the animal's neck onto the ground, as it continued to writhe, it's pathetic cries gurgling into silence as it drowned in its own blood.

"What type of disgusting, sick God would demand something like this?"

Still watching, he softly replied, "It's even more repulsive to him."

"Then why?"

"For *man's* disgusting sickness."

A moment passed as I pieced it together. "So this is like what, an offering for sin?"

"It's not our first choice."

"You've got something better?"

Still watching, he nodded and quietly answered, "Soon."

The animal stopped moving, except for occasional, involuntary jerks. Now there was only the stream of blood which the leader was collecting in a silver cup placed below the gaping wound.

Still watching, but sensing my revulsion, Yeshua asked, "Do you remember what you saw on that mountain top? All that light? All that purity?"

I nodded. "So much I couldn't stay on my feet."

"What would happen if all that purity was to embrace you? Enter you?"

I grudgingly continued the conversation. "I don't know, I guess I'd blow up."

"Because?"

"Because it's overwhelming."

"His purity, compared to yours."

"Of course," I said. He remained silent, knowing I'd take the bait. I didn't disappoint. "And killing some innocent animal is going to fix all that?"

"It's not the animal. It's the blood, the essence of his life. What you see are the impurities of those men's lives being transferred into his."

"And that's not obscene?"

"Sin is obscene."

"Why doesn't God just snap his fingers and make all the sin disappear?"

"Would you call that justice?" I had no answer and he continued. "God is not whimsical. The universe runs on logic, cause and effect. You jump off a cliff, you die. You sin, you pay."

I motioned to the animal. "So, he's picking up their tab."

"It's only a stop gap, until something better comes along."

"Instead of the blood of some helpless animal . . ."

He quietly answered, "It will be the blood of God."

I turned to stare at him. He continued to watch the proceedings as the priest reverently held up the cup of blood and walked slowly toward the building.

"Where's he going with it?" I asked.

"Inside to sprinkle it on the alter."

"Why there?"

"It's the holy place. Where God and man meet—until the new contract."

"And then?"

For the first time in our conversation he turned to me. Raising a hand, he reached out and gently tapped my chest. "The holy place will then be here."

The moment was broken by the sound of chopping. We turned our attention back to the animal. Four priests, one at each leg, were hacking away, dismembering them from the torso. Another had cut open the belly and was scooping out the intestines and organs. Two more started at the hind quarters where they were scraping and pulling back the skin.

Once again, sensing my disgust, he explained. "They'll roast it with fire—and then eat it."

As he spoke and I watched, an earlier saying of his surfaced in my mind. I softly quoted, "'Unless you eat my flesh and drink my blood . . .'"

He nodded. "I can only serve you the meal, Will. I can't make you eat."

Throughout the conversation, I felt my anger at his betrayal starting to fade. His compassion dissolving my resolution. If I didn't take a stand and hold my ground, things would slip back to where they were. And if this grotesque scene before us, this "eating of his flesh" was somehow designed to persuade me, it did just the opposite—assuring me more than ever, that my friend, miracle worker or not, compassionate or not—was someone I could not rely on. I looked at the ground, took a breath, and said, "And if I choose to eat and drink something else? If I decide on a different menu?"

"You'd choose to enter his presence with your impurities?"

"I have that choice, right? Free will?"

He looked back to the priests as they continued their chopping and skinning and gutting. Then, barely perceptibly, he began to nod. I turned to him, waiting for our eyes to meet. He deserved that much. When they did, his were already filled with sorrow over the words I was about to speak. But I would not be swayed. "Then—I guess you can count me out."

He nodded slowly, sadly.

Instantly, I was back in my sister's savings and loan, the sudden chill of the air conditioning causing me to shudder. Once again, I was able to break his spell. Was I torn? Of course. A close friendship had formed. But how many times can a friend, close or not, burn you, be unreliable, refuse to help even when you desperately need it? Would I miss his companionship? His insight? Of course. But it was time to draw the line. Time to regain control of my life.

EIGHTEEN

"YOU GOING TO be okay?"

"I'm fine."

"You can call me any time you want."

She said nothing.

"I'm serious."

More silence.

From the front door where Amber and I stood, I threw a look down the hallway to the dining room. The six or seven kids were already eating dinner. The house parents were there, somewhere, keeping an eye on them—and us. Not that we were running off together. A far cry from it.

Two days earlier, Child Welfare had swung by Hell House. For what, I wasn't entirely sure. I tried explaining the place was totally irrelevant but they were the State so, of course, they knew best. And for reasons even more irrational, Amber insisted upon spending all morning and half the afternoon trying to make the house look presentable. Terra was a terrible housekeeper and it appeared to be another genetic predisposition passed on to her daughter. Nevertheless, Amber was motivated to give it all she had.

"Maybe if we get it real clean, they'll let me stay."

"I don't think—"

"Yeah I know, the bank wants it, but you could sell your place, buy this and move back down here."

"I can't even visit this place without getting the creeps. No way am I going to—"

"Don't worry, we'll think of something." She slipped her headphones back on. "I'm going to the basement," she yelled, "to throw sheets over all the crap."

The social worker, a Dr. Alison, showed up at precisely 4:00—not 3:59, not 4:01—4:00. She was a stout woman of color, sweet and kind, neat as a pin. As she sat on the sofa, I was painfully aware of her view of the stained carpet, the chipped floorboards, and the brown water mark in the center of the ceiling resembling a giant Rorschach test.

Earlier, I'd used steam from the shower to smooth out the wrinkles in my shirt. Amber washed her hair and changed into a dress of her mother's to look strikingly mature. I sat in an old rocker and Amber chose the overstuffed chair with matching hand towels to cover the cigarette holes. Both of us hoped the smell of last-minute "Lysol-ing" the place had aired out.

Once the pleasantries were over, Dr. Alison pulled forms from her satchel and got down to business. "Looking over the paperwork," she said, "it's unfortunate your mother left no directive for your care."

"Oh, she did," Amber said. "Right, Uncle Will?"

"Well . . ."

The doctor turned to me. "She did?"

Amber cut in. "Oh, sure. Maybe not written down, but we always talked about it. You know, at Christmas, Thanksgiving, camping trips, all those family get-together times, right, Uncle Will?"

I tried to nod but wasn't nearly the con artist my niece was. The social worker clearly saw it but Amber was on a roll.

"We're hoping to buy the house back, you know, from the bank, lots of childhood memories, and all. But even if we can't, Uncle Will, he's a college professor you know, he has this real nice place on one of the islands up north, beachfront property and everything."

"I see." The woman smiled. "And what does Mrs. Thomas think of all of this?"

"Well—"

"There is no Mrs. Thomas," Amber cut in. "Which is why I do all the cooking and stuff when I'm up there. Real cozy, just the two of us. Oh, and Sigmund his dog and Sabrina the cat."

Dr. Alison nodded, quietly waiting for me to weigh in with a bit more reality. I took the cue. "Actually, Amber, we really haven't discussed that; you moving in with me, I mean."

"Sure we have. All the time."

"Not really."

And that's when the rift began. Not that we were great pals before but at that moment a giant chasm opened between us. We did our best to put on good faces, at least while the social worker was there, but it disappeared the moment the front door closed behind her.

"You don't want me to stay with you!" It was more accusation than question.

"I, uh . . ."

"What!"

"I'm not qualified," I said. "I have no experience raising a child."

"I'm not a child!" She motioned to her belly. "Or hadn't you noticed?"

"Exactly. And to add a baby into the—"

"I'll do it all, I can handle everything."

"Out on the island, all by yourself, when I'm at work? Sometimes the school's got night events and I have to sleep over. The ferry doesn't run that late and—"

"So, you don't want me!"

"I didn't say that."

"You don't have to."

"Amber—"

"It's Ambrosia. How many times do I have to tell you. *Ambrosia*."

"The point is—"

"I know all about your stupid points and I'm sick of them."

"What I'm—"

"The point is you don't want me to stay with you. Right?"

I hesitated.

"Right?"

It was the second hesitation that did it—the one trying to find a way of telling the truth without destroying her. She heard all the other truths—how I wasn't qualified, how I didn't know the first thing about raising a teenager. Or a baby. But in that brief second, she read a bigger truth: I didn't want to.

It's not that I disliked her, she was my niece, family. But all the drama, the schizophrenia, the attitude, the sense of entitlement, the demands . . . The point is, and yes there is a point, I could stand for a little peace. The last two weeks were a whirlwind, a category five hurricane, pulling me in every direction, often at the same time. So, yes, at least for the time being I could stand for a little peace. Later we could explore the possibilities.

Which brought us to now, forty-eight hours later, where we stood in the entry hall of the temporary foster home saying our goodbyes. At least I was saying them. "School's starting up but I'll be down next weekend, you know, to check up on you and everything."

Silence.

"You're family, Amber. We're all each other have."

She turned and looked down the hall to the dining room.

"And I see your point, I do. This will just give us a little time to catch our breath. Sort things out."

Still nothing.

"Okay?"

Finally, she spoke. "Are we done here?"

"Yeah, I uh, I guess we are." Knowing I should do something, create some sort of closure, I leaned over to give her a hug.

She stepped back. I nodded. I deserved that.

"Well—" I glanced down, buttoning my coat. "I guess I'll see you next week, then. In the meantime, if there's anything you . . ."

But when I looked back up, she was already moving down the hall.

"Okay then," I called.

I waited another moment then turned for the door. I hesitated, then looked back. She continued down the hall looking so small. Vulnerable. And, at that moment, I made a vow. I would always stay in touch with her. Whatever happened, I'd always stay in touch. But as for the details, technically it was out of my hands. Now, it was up to her and to the State.

With that feeble rationalization, I opened the door and stepped out into the cold drizzle.

NINETEEN

I WISH I could say the evening's ride up I-5 home was relaxing—thin traffic, gentle rain, the rhythmic swooshing of wipers. A return to peaceful, B.A. (Before Amber) solitude and, yes, I suppose, B.C. Not that Amber was all that noisy, at least physically, not with her cell phone and headphones. But sometimes her very presence filled the room as loud as if she was shouting.

Nevertheless, I couldn't shake that last image. The fragile, child/woman walking alone down the hallway. Just her and an unknown child growing inside her. Was she frightened? Terrified, I'm guessing. But of course she didn't show it. Like everyone else in our family she learned to deny and bury. Even at the tender age of fourteen, sorry, almost fifteen, she built her wall, that hidden place where she could safely live. Mom had her booze, I had my books, and Terra, her drugs, and boyfriends. Welcome to the family, little one.

I stretched the tightening cables in the back of my neck. The dashboard clock said it was a little after 10 p.m.

Actually, it was nine, since I never bothered changing it from Daylight Savings. (In a few months I'd just have to change it again.) I'd easily catch the last ferry and be home by eleven. Home. Just Siggy, myself—and Emily Dickinson. Snuggled cozily in my recliner, surrounded by the glass alcove encased in mist and fog. And the tide silently slipping in and out—always certain, always dependable.

The visitations had ceased. Why they started in the first place was still a mystery. But, once I took that final stand, I'd brought them to a close. No more intrusions, no more lessons, no more guilt. Well, two out of three wasn't bad. Because, no matter how I tried, I couldn't forget the image of my niece walking down that hallway.

But not alone. I made it clear to her we were family. I promised I'd regularly check in on her.

But that walk . . .

Maybe it wouldn't hurt to give her a call. Just to reassure her. She'd no doubt eaten by now and, who knows, maybe even made a friend. And even if she hadn't, even if she'd retreated back into her headphones, I knew she'd pick up. I never saw her refuse a call—at least the few that came in. She always answered then, of course, move out of earshot to carry on her conversations.

I pulled the phone from my coat pocket and, keeping an eye on the road, dialed her number. It rang four times before her voice mail kicked in:

"You know the drill." *Beep*.

"Hi. Hey, Amber. This is, um Uncle Will. Just checking in. When you get a chance, let me know how you're doin'. Kay? Thanks." I hung up, congratulating myself for going the extra mile. But it didn't stick. Why hadn't she picked up? She always picked up—unless she was on another line. I laid the phone on the seat and waited a reasonable two or three minutes before redialing.

The results were the same.

Odd. Surely, she saw my number. She'd have known it was. . . Oh, wait. Of course. She *did* see my number, which is why she didn't pick up. Well, if she thought she was punishing me, she had another thought coming. I wouldn't be put off that easily. Not by a sulking teenager. I tried a third time. Same results. There had to be some way to get through to her. Maybe if somebody else called. Somebody we both knew. Somebody like—Darlene. The two seemed to hit it off when they were planning the New Year's Eve Party, even did a little shopping together—not to mention sharing an eye roll or two over stupid things I said or did.

I wasn't thrilled calling her. She'd already helped by looking in on Siggy and Karl. Another favor would only make me more indebted to her. But Amber is family. So, I sucked it up, found Darlene's number, and dialed. She picked up. And, after the obligatory inquiries on how I was doing, and dealing, and feeling, and was I taking care of myself, she agreed to call Amber and ask her to call me back. It was a long shot, but I had another ninety minutes of drive time ahead.

Five minutes later Darlene called back.

I answered in the middle of the first ring. "Did you get her?"

"It took three tries until somebody picked up."

"Somebody?"

He said she couldn't come to the phone right now. That she was '*predisposed*.'"

"*Predisposed?* What does that mean?"

"That's what I asked him, and he said . . ." she hesitated.

"What? Darlene, what did he say?"

"He told me to go 'F' myself and hung up."

I frowned.

"What type of foster home is she staying at?" she asked.

My mind raced.

"Will?"

I tried to sound calm. "Was it a kid? An adult? Could you tell?"

"No. He had this really gravelly voice, though. And an accent, kinda like Rocky from the movies. Except for the lisp."

The phrase stopped me cold. "He had—a lisp?"

"Almost comical; trying to sound all macho and everything but with this lisp."

My gut tightened.

"Will? Are you there?"

"Yeah," I croaked.

She kept talking, but I barely heard. "Course, I tried to call back, a couple times, but of course she, he, never picked up. Oh, and one other thing."

I squinted at the road, trying to focus.

"I don't want to worry you or anything but, well, he sounded pretty looped."

"*Looped?*"

"You know, high."

I don't remember hanging up but I do remember the onslaught of car lights and horns as I veered hard to the right through multiple lanes, just barely making the exit. I hit the top of the ramp, turned left over the overpass, then left again, and raced down the entrance ramp back onto the freeway.

CHAPTER
TWENTY

EVERYTHING FOCUSED—streetlights, taillights, the sound of my wipers. I had no doubt who the Rocky voice with the lisp belonged to. How had they stay connected? Was he the one she talked to on the phone? Why hadn't I been more diligent, nosier?

I reached for my phone to call the foster home but fumbled it, dropping it between the seat and console. I reached for it, doing my best to keep my eyes on the road as I drove too fast with one hand, groping in the dark with the other. How could I have been so stupid? Everything about her cried out for someone. Anyone. The loneliness, the feelings she was abandoned. Forget feelings, it was a flat-out fact. Why else had she come knocking on my door? And when we failed to connect, when *I* failed—of course she'd try other people and other things. Just like her mother—and her grandmother.

A gasp broke the heightened sounds of traffic—so close I thought it my own. It came again. Choking. Struggling to breathe. I jerked my head to the passenger seat. Nothing. I checked the rearview mirror.

And then I was gone.

I'm standing on a jagged hill, wind and rain blowing into my face. In front of me, eye level, not four yards away, are a pair of bloody, mud-smeared feet—one on top of the other, grotesquely impaled with an iron spike. My gaze shoots up the legs shiny with blood, past the naked genitals of a man, beyond his heaving, lacerated chest, until they finally rest upon the swollen, beaten face of—

"No!" I shouted. "No!

I was back in my car, still groping for the phone. I had stopped these visions before and they would stay stopped. Especially now. I felt the corner of the phone under the seat, used my fingertips to coax it closer, until I could finally scoop it into my hand. I glanced up just in time to see a big rig looming in front of me. I hit the brakes and slid, barely staying in my lane. I glanced at the speedometer. It read 84.

Easing back and vowing to watch the traffic more carefully, I flipped through the directory on my phone until I found the number and hit *dial*.

The foster home picked up on the second ring. "Johnson residence."

"Hi, I need you to check on uh—This is Will Thomas. I dropped my niece, Amber, Ambrosia off this evening and—

"Hello, Mr. Thomas.

"Hi, uh."

"This is Brenda Johnson."

"Oh, hi, Brenda. Listen, would you mind checking up on Amber for me?"

"Checking up?"

"Yeah, I've been calling and—"

"It's nearly 11:00. Everyone's in bed. We have a light's out polic—"

"Right, I appreciate that. But I'm not, I don't think— Would you mind checking? See if she's in bed?"

"Mr. Thomas."

"I'm not being overly protective here, I just, would you mind checking?"

"The first few nights are always the hardest."

"Right. Would you mind checking? There's a chance she's in trouble."

"Trouble?"

"Please, would you mind?"

A pause. Then, "All right. I have your number. I'll call you back if there's a—"

"I can hang on."

"I have your number. If there's a problem, I'll call you back. I promise."

"Okay. Right." I gripped the phone a little tighter. "But uh . . ."

"Yes?"

"Would you hurry? I think it may be urgent."

"I will."

"And, uh . . ."

"I'll call back If there's an issue, but I'm sure everything is just fine."

"Right, but—"

"Good night, Mr. Thomas."

"Good—"

She disconnected.

My speed had crept up to 80. I dropped back down and forced myself to take a deep, measured breath. But the guilt kept growing, the familiar pressure around my chest tightening. How many times could I have been there for her? How many times could we have talked? Of course, she played aloof, she was a teenager. But I'd broken through harder cases at school. All it took was persistence. Why hadn't I put in more effort? Why hadn't I—

Suddenly, I'm out of the car walking the beach below my house. Siggy is barking and bounding ahead. I glance through the mist up to the house where Amber stands watching from the window. Alone.

Why had I never invited her to join us?

"Please . . ."

I'm back on the hill, staring up at the face. His hair and beard are matted in blood. His nose broken. Blood bubbles from his mouth where teeth have been. One eye is crimson, the other swollen shut. He hangs on outstretched arms, his body collapsed upon itself making it impossible to breathe. I watch in horror as he fights to push himself up on those broken feet to suck in a breath. And then, never taking that blood-filled eye off me, he cries, *"Friend!"*

Now I'm back at my house, the living room, arguing with Amber.

"All I'm asking is—"

"I heard you the first time."

"Then at least have the courtesy to—"

"How 'bout *you* having some courtesy?"

"All I'm asking if for you to cut down on your time in the shower. There's nothing—"

"Like you're going to run out of water."

"It's not the—"

"We live on a whole ocean or hadn't you noticed?"

"Amber—"

I was back in the car again, shaking my head. Seriously? One of the few times she was out from under her headphones and that's when I chose to talk about wasting water?

Suddenly, I'm at the kitchen door declining Amber's offer to go shopping with her and Darlene.

"C'mon," Darlene coaxes, "it'll be fun."

"Thanks, but no. I have far too many papers to correct."

"Which will still be here when you get back.

"I don't think—"

"If he doesn't want to go, he doesn't want to go," Amber says as she brushes past me to the door. But even then, beneath her disdain, I hear the hurt. And I do nothing. What is wrong with me? What would a couple hours cost?

Back in the car, it grew harder to breathe as if weight was piled on top of my chest. How could I have been so selfish, so self-absorbed? Granted, she outclassed me in both departments but I was the grown-up, the one she came to. And the one who pushed her right into the arms of some pedophile bottom feeder.

I took the Northgate exit and gave Siri the address for the foster home. I knew how to get there, but with the thoughts, the guilt, and the visions continuing to come so vividly and fast, it was safer to just follow directions. I took another breath and—

"Friend . . ."

I'm back on the hill. The wind stronger, blowing my hair, snapping my clothes. I hear others around us but I pay no attention. I watch in horror as he pushes himself up again, his whole body trembling, fighting for breath. The blood, the beatings, tear at my heart. I can't just stand there; I have to help.

"What do I do?" I shout against the wind. "Tell me!"

Before he can answer, he collapses, the air squeezing from his lungs in a pathetic, ragged wheeze.

"Tell me!"

"Turn left one quarter mile and the destination will be on your left." I was back in the car, listening to Siri. I swiped at my eyes, struggling to breathe, myself. And then I saw it. Parked on a street to my right. A 1970's VW van covered in hippie flowers. I slammed on the brakes, threw the car into reverse, backed up, and turned to investigate.

Siri responded, "Calculating alternate route."

My heart hammered as I pulled beside the van. On its side panel was the painting of a leopard. I leaped from my car, leaving the door open and the alarm chiming.

"Hey!" I raced to the driver's side. The kid was leaning against the door as if asleep. I grabbed the handle and flung it open.

Suddenly awake, he struggled not to fall out. "What the—"

I spotted her across the seat on the passenger side, passed out. "Amber!"

"It's cool man, she's—"

I ran to the other side and threw open her door. "Amber!"

"She's cool, man."

I took her face in my hands. "Amber!" She gave no response. "Amber, can you hear me?"

"It's all good."

I fumbled for my phone.

"It's cool, man, everything's—"

Shut up!

Holding her with one hand, I thumb dialed with the other, trembling so violently, it took three tries. When I finally connected a voice, sounding more auto-pilot than human answered, "9-1-1, what is the nature of your emergency?"

"My niece!" I shouted. "She's overdosed!"

CHAPTER

TWENTY-ONE

THE EMS ARRIVED within minutes. Or maybe hours. Hard to know real time with everything happening because—

I'm suddenly standing in the hallway of Hell House two days earlier, watching Amber lying on her mother's bed, clutching her pillow, sobbing into it. And what do I do? Nothing. I stand there. A lost, little girl is grieving over her mother's death and I just stand there.

"Please . . ."

I'm back on the hill, rain pelting my face, as the macabre figure again gasps for breath. I have no idea how to help. But his feet, they're right there in front of me. I stumble through the mud and grab hold of the single spike grotesquely protruding through them. It's cold and slick with rain and with blood which, as with the animal sacrifice I witnessed earlier, has a faint, copper smell. I pull and tug at it. Nothing.

"No!" he cries.

I plant my feet and pull harder. It's driven too deep into the flesh and wood.

"NO!"

I look up and shout, "I don't understand!"

"There's nothing to understand, sir." It's a pudgy EMS attendant, his face flashing orange and red in the light. I stood watching as he and his partner slide Amber into the back of the vehicle. "It's company policy, you cannot ride with us."

I caught a glimpse of Amber before they shut the doors. If she was breathing, I couldn't tell.

"Follow in your car if you like and we'll meet you there."

"Is she going to be okay?"

"We'll meet you at the hospital."

I nodded, my feet frozen, as the attendant headed for the cab of the ambulance. "Wait!" I called. "What hospital?"

"Saint John's."

My gut tightened. It's the same hospital I'd last seen Terra. I turned from the EMS and saw I'd been joined by two squad cars. "Rocky with the Lisp" was leaning against the first and by the look of things he'd be well taken care of. I crossed to my car, the door alarm still sounding. I dropped into the front seat and reached to close the door when—

I see Mom, alive, passed out on the sofa. Terra is around eleven, I'm nine. We giggle as we rifle through her purse looking for money, until—

I'm in the back seat of Dad's borrowed Ford Galaxy—a high school junior, clumsily practicing sexual gymnastics with Sarah Postmen. Sweet, innocent Sarah, a willing participant but only because it will keep me, her jerk of a boyfriend, satisfied. It's no Me-Too moment but close enough to pile on more self-loathing.

"Mine!" his voice cries.

I shook my head and I'm back in my own car following the EMS's flashing lights. If I thought I'd lost my mind before, there was no doubt about it now. But that was my niece up ahead and crazy or not, as long as I could stay on the road, I'd follow.

I blink and I'm in ICU Cubicle 8, watching Amber as she stares at the wall, the floor, anywhere but at her dying mother. And what am I doing? Nothing. No arm around her, no words of consolation—just me wallowing in my own self-pity.

Back in the car, I gasped for air. It was getting harder to breathe as the guilt kept tightening.

It's afternoon. I'm on my way to Hell House, turning right on 15th Ave. I spot a homeless guy with a shopping cart and instinctively press auto lock.

"What are you doing?" Amber asks.

"Just a precaution."

"The sign says he needs money."

"Maybe he should try working for it."

"Please . . ."

I release my hold on the spike and grab the large, rough beam sunk into the ground. I use my shoulders to push against the wood. It won't budge. I wrap my arms around it and pull, my face inches from the slick, bloody calves where I now smell urine. But the beam, will not move.

I spot three men, soldiers, kneeling, throwing dice. I race to them, shouting, "Stop this! You don't know what you're doing!" But they don't hear. I reach out and grab the closest, but my hands pass through him. I try again. He's like a ghost. Vapor. Or maybe it's me. I try a third time. Again, in vain. I look back up and shout into the driving rain. "What am I supposed to do!"

He pushes up on his broken feet, writhing at the effort, until he can breathe and cries, *"My glory!"*

Suddenly I'm in fifth grade, wearing a T-shirt and P.E. shorts. I've joined the other guys in class taunting Tom Peterson over his club foot. It lasts only a moment before I'm six years old, stooping over ants with a magnifying glass, frying them on the sidewalk. Now I'm nine, at Safeway, slipping a Three Musketeers bar under my shirt. Eight. Throwing blackberries against the white wall of Haggen's house. The images come faster. High school library, writing a paper, copying word for word from the encyclopedia. In Michael Germain's bedroom, eagerly devouring his *Playboy*. Nothing ties together. Nothing except the growing, suffocating guilt.

"I bought them . . ." he chokes, before collapsing.

I wipe my face, barely able to see through the wind, the rain, and my tears. "Bought?" It's impossible to breathe, but I push out the word, "What?"

I'm in my college dorm accepting money writing essays for jocks. Having dry heaves at some frat party. Waking in bed with a wasted girl whose name I don't know.

The images are shattered by his ragged gasp, *"Mine!"*

I'm lost as moments roar in, tumbling over each other—the minor and unseen hit-and-run in the parking lot—embellishing a résumé—humiliating a slacker student for class levity—ignoring Siggy's business on the neighbor's front yard—belittling Cindy's intelligence—standing in the cave holding out the stone saying, "If you're really God's son—"

The hospital speed bumps jarred me back to the present or whatever was left of it. I spotted the EMS drivers unloading Amber and skidded to a stop. I jumped out and ran toward them. The glass doors hissed open as they entered. I barely managed to squeeze past, before they shut.

"Sir," the pudgy attendant ordered, "the waiting room is through the other entrance."

Without a word, I gripped the gurney's rail. Discussion closed.

We reached a curtained ER area where a doctor waited. She glanced to the attendants then to me. The look on my face made it clear there was no negotiating. I would not depart. Unfortunately, neither would my guilt.

I'm on break in the teacher's lounge, refusing to pick up Terra's call—ignoring her birthday on the fridge calendar—too busy to visit during her relapses—refusing her requests for loans—

"My—glory!" he gasps.

I can no longer breathe. I shake my head side to side like a wounded animal.

"Your failures!"

"I don't—"

"My glory!" He collapses again, suffocating.

I lean over my knees, fighting to breathe.

He pushes on his feet, face twisting in pain. *"I paid for them!"*

"What do you—"

"Give to me!"

"I don't—"

"My glory—give to me!" he cries and collapses.

That's when it hits me. He's not asking for my help, he's asking for—my guilt.

"Sir?" I hear a nurse speaking, "you'd better sit down."

I'm wheezing, no air will come.

She eases me into a chair near the wall. "Please take a seat."

"I paid!" he gasps.

I'm crying, unable to breathe in the wind and rain. "You can't—"

"My glory!"

"I—"

"Give to me!"

"What—what am I supposed—"

"Mine!"

I choke, arguing, "It's *my* sin."

"I paid!"

My knees turn to rubber, my legs no longer hold my weight. I cannot stand before the spectacle in front of me, his pain, his anguish, his plea. I drop into the mud in silent sobs.

He cries out, more air than words. *"Give me my glory!"*

And there, sitting in the ER room before my dying niece, kneeling in the mud before my tortured friend, I begin to nod. I feel a faint, warm mist. Almost imperceptible. I don't open my eyes; I don't have to. I know it's the wind. I know it's spraying blood over me. Sprinkling his blood upon my alter.

"Yes," I finally manage a whisper, "yes." And each time I speak the word, the crushing weight on my chest grows lighter, my breathing easier. "Yes . . ."

How long I remained there, sitting in the chair, kneeling in the mud? Two hours. Two minutes. Again, no idea—until the doctor spoke to me.

"Mr. Thomas?" I looked up to see her motioning to Amber. "She wants to speak to you."

I glanced about. Another vision?

"Mr. Thomas?"

"Yes!" I blurted, then jumped to my feet so fast my head spun.

"Whoa." The doctor took my arm. "Are you going to be all right?

"Yes," I said, taking another breath. "Yes." I turned to Amber whose eyes were still closed. "Is she . . ."

"She won't be feeling any pain for a while, but she's definitely out of the—"

I broke past her, stumbling to the bed rail. "Amber . . ."

The doctor joined me. "Did you know she's pregnant?"

I nodded, staring down at her, reaching out and gently taking her hand. Her eyes remained closed. But her lips began to move. She was trying to speak.

"Amber?" I leaned down.

It was a breathy whisper, so faint I had to put my ear next to her mouth.

"What? What did you say?"

She repeated the words and I broke into a smile.

"What did she say?" the doctor asked.

I swallowed back the emotion. "She said . . ." I gave my eyes a swipe. "She said, 'My name is Ambrosia.'"

TWENTY-TWO

"COOL, THE SUN'S out," Amber said as we stood on the ferry's deck looking out over the water. "You can actually see the islands."

I nodded, taking a sip of my coffee. "Still pretty cold, though."

"Is there anything you don't complain about?"

"I'm sorry?"

Still looking over the water, she said, "You've really got to develop a better attitude."

"*I've* got to—"

"There's a whole world out there. Try not being so negative and experience it a little."

I started to answer but knew she'd just wear me down. Part of her M.O. It didn't matter whether she was right or wrong, as long as she kept the argument going, she considered it a win. And when she grew weary, she'd just slip on those pink headphones and consider another point scored.

Clever creatures, these teen girls.

I looked out to one of the islands. The Native Americans say when the Creator scooped out Puget Sound with his hand, the San Juan Islands were what slipped between his fingers. Maybe so. Or maybe we just thought they slipped through his fingers. Maybe each one was intentional. Maybe we all were. What did Yeshua say, "When you're infinite, everyone is his favorite kid."

While waiting for Amber's release from the hospital, I spent the time at Hell House. My department head wasn't crazy about my missing the first days of the new semester and let slip that, after the New Year's party, it may be the least of my worries. I stuck around for two more meetings with Dr. Alison, our case worker. One at the house and one at her office.

After carefully reviewing the options and with Amber's permission, it was agreed Amber could come back home with me on a temporary basis. After further evaluation, including visits to the house and some counseling, if we still agreed, we could explore an extended trial or even permanent basis.

The ferry's PA boomed, "We'll be docking in ten minutes. Drivers, please return to your vehicles. Docking in ten minutes."

"Think the car is aired out yet?" I asked. It was supposed to be a joke but was met with the vintage Amber sigh of insufferable endurance. My point was we had filled the trunk and piled the back seat with all of her clothes and many of her mother's. With no workable washing machine and since several surpassed the limits of human hygiene, to save money, we (i.e., Amber) figured we'd wait to use mine. A logical choice except for the two-hour drive in a closed car during the dead of winter.

We turned from the ferry's railing and headed for the car when Amber's phone chimed. She saw my micro-flinch of concern and responded with an eye roll as she answered it. "Hey." She turned to console me. "It's just Aunt Darlene."

I coughed on my coffee. *"Aunt?"*

"She wants to know when we'll get there. Says dinner is getting cold."

"Dinner?"

Amber spoke back into the phone: "About twenty minutes." Then to me: "Wouldn't you say twenty minutes?"

I numbly nodded. And for the hundredth time found myself wondering what journey I'd signed up for.

"It really is."

I blinked and saw I was standing next to a small fire on a beach. Yeshua kneeled nearby, frying a half dozen fish over the flames.

"Oh," I said, taking a moment to get my bearings. "Hey."

"Hey." He poked at a couple fish and flipped others over. "It really is a journey, isn't it? Quite a voyage."

I didn't know how to respond. It had been several days since our last encounter. And I was still haunted by the gruesome event I saw him go through. Kneeling to join him, I said, "I see you made it."

He nodded. "A little worse for wear, but yeah."

"Listen," I said. "I feel awful about all that. I'm so sorry—"

"You're not feeling guilty, are you?"

"I—"

"You're not trying to steal my glory again?"

"No, no. I—"

"Thanks," he said, rising to his feet. "I paid a lot for that."

"Sure," I said, "Any time."

He cut me a look then shaded his eyes against the morning sun to scan the adjacent lake. Two hundred yards away, a fishing boat was working the waters. "The boys are still out there," he said.

"Your disciples?"

He nodded. "They'll be starting their own journey soon enough." I stood to join him as he continued. "They haven't quite gotten it yet, but they will."

"Gotten it?" I asked.

"That it's the voyage we care about—not the destination."

"I don't—"

"They think, all the problems they're going to run into are supposed to be solved."

"They're not?"

"Oh, they will be. But the real purpose is not to solve the problem, it's to change the person. We talked about that, right? Problems are just the vehicle. Solving them is not the destination."

"And the destination is . . ."

"You."

"Me?"

"Of course. Listen, you don't have any more of those balloon things, do you?"

"So," I continued the thought, "the destination is equalizing the pressure to overcome the problems."

"You're not listening," he said. "It's not about overcoming problems."

"Then—"

"It's about increasing our presence. It's about making you like us. Whole. Complete. Not lacking anything. It's who you become during the voyage."

"And the voyage, that's what we live out down here?"

"And not just here." He kneeled back to the fire.

"You mean . . ."

"You think the process stops at death?"

"Well, I just figured . . ."

"Kinda makes all of this here useless then, doesn't it? All the suffering, the growing pains—why bother if everyone's suddenly changed anyway."

"In the twinkling of an eye," I said. "Isn't that from the Bible?"

"Absolutely. But that's your body, not your soul."

"And my soul?"

"Just keeps growing—for eternity."

I paused, carefully weighing what he said. Then, kneeling to join him, I asked what had been on my mind ever since Terra's death. "What about, you know, my sister?"

"You think I ignored your prayer."

"Well—you didn't answer it."

"I didn't?"

I frowned.

"You asked me to heal her."

"By killing her?"

"She killed herself." He added a few sticks to the fire, then sighed heavily. "Free will."

"Right, right—but she would never have done that if she knew she was headed to, if she knew she was going to . . ."

"Hell?" he asked.

I looked away.

"Do you really think something like that would prevent her from being with us?"

I wasn't sure how to answer.

"Hell," he repeated, his voice growing soft with sadness. "It's simply letting people have what they want."

"Free will," I repeated, growing less and less fond of the word.

"It breaks our heart, but if our children don't want us . . ." He shook his head. I watched as his sadness grew.

Finally, I asked, "My sister, she wasn't exactly what you'd call a Believer."

He turned to me. "Says who? You?"

"Well—you saw her life."

He took nearby bread and carefully laid it close enough to the flames to warm but not burn it. Only then did I see the gaping wound in each of his hands. "Will," he said, "do you remember that picture I drew at the hospital? The one with the throne and the addict prostitute?"

I felt my jaw slack. "That was Terra?"

"What direction do you suppose your sister was facing?"

I hesitated. "Toward the throne, toward you?"

"She had her baggage, all those wars raging inside her heart, all that self-hatred. But there was a part of her that was always turned to us."

"She turned—" my voice thickened. "She turned to you?"

He nodded. "She always wanted our love, our friendship."

I looked to the ground, trying to digest the information. "She did?"

"And she has it." I felt his hand rest on my shoulder. "Not the way we wished, but she has more than you can possibly imagine."

When I looked back into his face, he was smiling. I wiped my eyes and tried returning it. "You know," I coughed slightly, "if someone were to write all of this stuff down into a book, it could really change things."

"Change things?"

"Yeah, for my generation, our entire culture. It could really start a revival."

"A revival?" Instead of excitement, he sounded a little disappointed.

"What? You don't want a revival?"

He looked back out over the water, sadly shaking his head. "I'm not sure a revival will do any good."

"What then?" I repeated. "What do you want?"

He turned back, looking into me with those deep, compassionate eyes. "I was hoping for a reformation."

"Uncle Will, look?"

I was back on the ferry. We'd just stepped onto the car level and mine was just ahead. As we approached, I saw through the open window something in the back seat. So did Amber. She picked up her pace to investigate.

"Amber, be care—"

She arrived and reached for the passenger door. After opening it, all she said was, "Cool."

I joined her as she pulled out an arrangement of helium-filled balloons—about half a dozen, all different colors.

"What on earth?" I looked all around to see who might be responsible. None of the drivers returning to their cars seemed to notice or care.

"There's a message." Amber reached for a small envelope attached to the heavy fishing lure holding them down. She opened it and silently read.

"What's it say?" I asked.

"How weird."

"Amber?"

She looked across the hood to me.

"Well?"

She frowned then read only two words: "Bon Voyage."

Soli Deo gloria

Rendezvous with GOD
Volume One

DISCUSSION QUESTIONS

CHAPTER ONE

These first few questions are just a warm-up. Trust me, they get deeper and more personal as we continue our journey with Will. But for now:

1. Putting on our psychology hats for a moment, what would you say is Will's greatest problem? Loneliness? Cindy's betrayal? Cats?

2. Does he even know there is a problem?

3. Do you see any similarities in your own life? In the lives of specific friends or family?

4. There's plenty to untangle here and no overnight solutions, but if you were a passionate God concerned with every detail of Will's life, what would you do? Where would you start his recovery?

5. Finally, what's the deal with Ambrosia? On the surface she appears to be just another trial to get through. What are the Ambrosias (human or situational) in your own life?

CHAPTER TWO

The Bible doesn't give much insight regarding Jesus's childhood. However, Hebrews 5:8–9 does say:

> *Son though he was, he learned obedience from what he suffered and, once made perfect, he became the source of eternal salvation for all who obey him.*

So, we know there was a growth process. This doesn't mean he sinned but it does mean in growing up he "learned obedience" and was "made perfect" by what he suffered.

1. With that in mind, why was the boy, Yeshua, crying?

2. How was his suffering similar to Will's?

Back to Hebrews; verse 2:18 says this about Jesus:

> *Because he himself suffered when he was tempted, he is able to help those who are being tempted.*

What a comfort to know Jesus totally relates to our suffering when we're tempted, because he came down and faced it.

That said:

3. Besides feeling the same pain as Will, what was Yeshua's solution to his problem?

4. Yeshua explains that Will was created so God could enjoy him as a father enjoys his children. In the Gospels, Jesus turned the religious community upside down by instructing us to address the unapproachable Yahweh as an intimate, "Father." This in no way lowers God's position, but

raises ours, demonstrating to us how deeply valuable he sees each of us. What are your thoughts about referring to the sovereign God and Creator as Father?

5. If we really believed, I mean *REALLY* believed the Creator of the Universe is our deeply caring father and we are his greatly loved children—how would that affect our self-image? How would that impact our relationship with him?

6. How would such a belief free you to put aside fear of every kind and live life at full throttle?

CHAPTER THREE

The scene between Yeshua and Joseph still chokes me up a little—the bittersweet joy of seeing my precious, little child change to become a strong, self-sufficient adult. It really is the second cutting of the cord. And in the process, as Yeshua points out, every day teens are a little different than who they were the day before, making it difficult for either side to keep up.

For those who have gone, will go, or are currently entering this transitional phase:

1. Was there a time you gave your teen too much freedom? Too little freedom? Explain.

2. Did it permanently scar them as adults?

It seemed as my wife and I raised our teens, we had to remind ourselves a dozen times a week—it's not the issues of the particular conflict that count—but the relationship. And that relationship will last forever.

That's why love and forgiveness are so vital. As the perfect Son of God, I'm sure Jesus's temptation to correct Joseph and Mary was constant. But love and mercy pulled him through. Not that we can expect such divine behavior from our own kids. But as adults, we can try to understand their real or imaginary frustrations and ask for God's love and forgiveness to fill in where theirs may be momentarily missing.

But letting go isn't just for teens and parents. In the final section, Yeshua points out that free will is one of God's greatest gifts. And yet:

3. Can free will become a burden? How?

4. What would happen if there was no free will, if we (or our teens) were never in a position to make mistakes?

CHAPTER FOUR

Yeshua talks about the Old Contract (Testament) versus the New Contract (Testament). The difference between them is huge, but since both are written by the same God and are in the same Book, we often mix them together, seeing them as one.

1. How would you define the differences between the Old and New contracts?

I was astonished to read that Jesus said John the Baptist was least in the Kingdom of God. But he's quoted as saying that very thing in both Matthew 11:11 and here in Luke 7:28:

> *"I tell you, among those born of women there is no one greater than John; yet whoever is least in the kingdom of God is greater than he."*

When it comes to a man born of woman there is no one greater than John. By his own man-made power, his goodness and devotion to God is unsurpassed. Still, that's by his own power. But for those who have entered the Kingdom of God through the New Contract:

    A. Our failures are completely forgiven through Christ's sacrifice.

    B. We are new creatures. Unlike John or even the scribes and Pharisees, we no longer have to struggle on our own to fulfill our side of the contract. We are now empowered by the Holy Spirit. With his power, our cooperation, and Christ's sacrifice we actually become far greater and more holy than anyone under the Old Contract.

And what do we have to do to enter this New Contract? Simply sign it with our belief. Again, the difference is HUGE—and the very thing separating Christianity from any other philosophy or religion. Instead of trying to modify our characters through our own power, we ask God to come in and SUPERNATURALLY transform us.

3. What does Yeshua say is the difference between character modification and spiritual transformation?

4. In what ways does religion without relationship kill?

5. In 2 Corinthians 3:6 what did Paul mean when he wrote, *"He has made us competent as ministers of a new covenant—not of the letter but of the Spirit; for the letter kills, but the Spirit gives life."*

6. Why are we tempted to fall back into following religious rules instead of pursuing a living relationship? In what ways are following rules easier than having a relationship? In what ways harder?

CHAPTER FIVE

I'm not a fan of fasting. Missing a few meals is a miserable experience that lowers my blood sugar, fogs my thinking, and makes me cranky. Still, before I start a novel, I usually go off somewhere and subject myself to this misery. Why? Mostly because Jesus seemed to think it was a good idea. Does it help my writing? Who knows? I've never felt super-inspired or seen a burning rose bush or received an angel-gram.

But there was one time that still makes me smile. I spent all day "suffering" and, as usual, got nothing in return except a headache. I walked back to the car grumbling about another wasted day when it suddenly dawned on me: I spent the entire time asking God to help me write what I wanted to say and not once did I bother asking him if *he* had anything to say. I literally burst out laughing at my idiocy (one of God's and my favorite past times) and apologized saying, "I'm sorry, is there, by chance, anything you'd like to add?"

Whoosh, thoughts came flooding into my mind. I remember digging into my pocket for pen and paper and giggling, "Wait a minute, hold on, give me a second!" as I began scribbling notes. Notes that became the backbone of one of my favorite novels, *Fire of Heaven*. Does it happen every time? I wish. But is it possible invisible things just as powerful happen that he doesn't bother to inform me about? That's certainly my prayer.

Moving on.

It's interesting Jesus was not sent into the desert to be tempted until the Father clearly proclaimed his identity. Only then was he ready to be tested. And what were the tests? Each time they were questioning his identity:

> "IF you are the Son of God . . . PROVE IT by what you do (turning these stones to bread)."

> "IF you are the Son of God . . . PROVE IT by what the temple priests will say about you (when they see angels catching you)."

> "IF you are the Son of God . . . PROVE IT by what you own (when I give you all the world)."

Henri Nouwen points out how these false perceptions are the same ones tempting us today. Instead of seeing our identity through God's eyes, as his beloved children, we are seduced into judging ourselves as the world judges; thinking we're only as good as:

- What we accomplish.
- What other people say about us.
- What we own.

If we buy into these false values, which constantly fluctuate, our peace as his children is replaced by worry, strife, and depression.

With that in mind—

1. What specific ways are you tempted to prove your worth by what you do?

2. What specific ways are you tempted to prove your value by what others say about you?

3. What specific ways are you tempted to prove your worth by what you have?

Of course, the sad fact is many of us waste our entire life trying to prove our value by chasing after momentary counterfeits—instead of resting in the peace and joy of the Creator who adores each of us as his favorite child.

CHAPTER SIX

I used to hate the silence of God. I thought those seasons came because of some failure on my part. What's the old saying, "If God is distant, maybe you're the one who moved away?" Or maybe, as in the story when Will was dumping out all the booze, I figured I wasn't being religious enough. Eventually, I understood these silent times are the most valuable. Like a tree in time of drought, they force me to sink my roots deeper in search for him—strengthening my faith root-system, allowing me to withstand great windstorms for myself and for others.

1. Have you ever experienced the silence of God? If he doesn't address an immediate concern, is it possible he's dealing with something even more important—like your faith?

2. Is there a past example in your life?

Moving on.

When Jesus first announced his mission in Luke 4:18, he quoted a passage from Isaiah and said it was actually about him:

> *"He has sent me to proclaim freedom for the prisoners . . . to set the oppressed free."*

Oppressed? By what? Another time, he not only chose to perform his first miracle at a celebration, but chose it to be changing 180 gallons of water into fine wine (albeit a lower alcohol content than today's).

3. But why? What statement was he making?

We know God is not advocating joy through drunkenness and yet our joy seems incredibly important to him. In fact, the word "joy" appears in the Bible around 200 times.

4. How do we live in holiness without becoming uptight and religiously self-righteous? What misconception does the world have when it views Jesus (and his followers) as "buzzkills"?

Finally, regarding the metaphor of the wick in the oil lamp—

5. Instead of burning ourselves up in service and obedience to God, how do we keep ourselves saturated in his Spirit so it's actually his Spirit that burns?

CHAPTER SEVEN

Instead of trying to fix a problem by bringing it to God, Yeshua suggests bringing God into the problem.

1. What does that mean? What's the difference between begging God to fix the Amber problems of our lives, instead of bringing him into them? How would that change our outlook? How would that change our prayers?

When first-century Christians were persecuted and tortured to death, James, who headed up the church from Jerusalem, wrote this in James 1:2–4:

> *Consider it pure joy, my brothers and sisters, whenever you face trials of many kinds, because you know that the testing of your faith produces perseverance. Let perseverance finish its work so that you may be mature and complete, not lacking anything.*

How revolutionarily different that is from suggesting they beg God to deliver them from their troubles? Instead, James suggests they change their mind-set from pleading for God to stop the troubles to actually embracing the idea he will use those troubles to accomplish greater purposes—maybe not outside the person, but inside. He doesn't even suggest a compromise of some self-pitying response like, "I guess this is my lot, so I'll have to accept it." Instead, he says to consider it— "*PURE JOY.*"

This brings us to the balloon illustration—God filling us with his presence to push back on all of today's outside pressures. What if troubles are not about us being the victims but are actually opportunities to seek more of his Spirit inside us to push back?

2. If that's the case, how is the storm the disciples are about to face actually a blessing instead of a difficulty?

3. How does this apply to the difficulties you're currently facing?

CHAPTER EIGHT

While everyone else sees the demon-possessed madman as someone to fear and chain up, Yeshua sees him through entirely different eyes. He doesn't deal with him as his enemy but as a prisoner of war. What a major shift in thinking.

1. What would happen if we viewed every personal enemy like that? What would happen to us? What would happen to them?

A cornerstone in my life is the belief God never plays defense. Never. This probably comes from the first Bible verse I memorized, Romans 8:28:

> *And we know that in all things God works for the good of those who love him, who have been called according to his purpose.*

2. What if the above verse is actually true? What if the apostle Paul wasn't exaggerating when he wrote it? Would we run away from ugly situations and people or would we race toward them with eager anticipation?

Frightening? You bet. As frightening as facing down a crazy demoniac—and setting him free.

CHAPTER TEN

Yeshua tells Will not to fret over his last debacle by insisting God's brightest victories happen in the darkest places. He then points out examples from the Bible.

1. Are there past examples of this in your own life? Are you currently facing some "darkest places"?

Will points out when Jesus started accumulating a large following, he'd say something that thinned the crowd.

2. What was Jesus's reasoning? Are we expected to follow his example when it comes to our own programs for the Kingdom of God—like churches, Bible studies, personal witnessing?

Like Jairus, I sometimes feel God has forgotten his promises to me—or he has missed the moment. And yet, by going the distance with God's promise, even when it appeared hopeless, Jairus not only wound up with a greater miracle but Jesus wound up more glorified.

3. How do we believe when God seems unbelievable?

CHAPTER TWELVE

Again and again we read of the people in Jesus's day, including the disciples, trying to reduce his choices to their limited understanding of a situation. Is it A or is it B? Is it yes or no? On/off. Attempts to reduce an infinite God into one who is binary. That's why I seldom answer hypothetical questions. They cut out the God Factor. They limit the possibility of him doing something crazy, off the charts, and—supernatural.

1. Consider one or two times in Scripture when God's response came out of left field (or higher dimensional thinking).

Moving on. In Romans 5:8, Paul writes:

> *But God demonstrates his own love for us in this:*
> *While we were still sinners, Christ died for us.*

2. How does this verse apply to Yeshua's diagram of repentance?

3. Is there a danger of the "junkie prostitute" continuing to remain in her sins?

4. Is there a danger of Mr. "Club Christ" remaining in his sins?

And so, we're back to the radical concept of character modification versus spiritual transformation.

5. If both remain facing their current direction—the prostitute facing Jesus, the club member facing away—who will eventually be transformed?

CHAPTER THIRTEEN

1. Why are events forcing Will to return to the place of his nightmare?

Some hold to an interesting theory regarding Job 3:25:

> *"What I feared has come upon me; what I dreaded*
> *has happened to me."*

Since God never wastes the sorrow of his children, some suggest he allowed Satan to attack in the areas Job feared most—not to make him suffer more, but to prove to Job he could face them—so he would no longer be enslaved by his fear of them.

2. What fears enslave you most? What terrors rob you of the abundant life Jesus promises?

In the story, it appears Yeshua is beginning some deep surgery and healing into areas crippling Will for decades. Unforgiveness is at the top of the list—not only for Will, but for many of us. It's interesting in the Lord's Prayer, as brief as it is, Jesus made a huge point of forgiveness, literally telling us to ask the Father to forgive us *AS* we forgive others.

3. Is there somebody you've not entirely forgiven? Having trouble thinking of someone? Double-check with the Holy Spirit and see if there's anyone he'd reveal to you.

There was a man I could not forgive. I knew I should and I tried but I just kept failing, my anger churning and roiling inside, to the point of getting my first (and last) ulcer. I pleaded and pleaded with the Lord for help—until I remembered his command to pray for my enemies. I certainly didn't want to practice it, but anything was better than my torment. So, I began praying for him, often through gritted teeth; not for God to smite him or show him the error of his ways, but for God to (*gulp*) bless him. Eventually, not overnight, but within a few weeks my hatred and unforgiveness began to dissolve until I was no longer the man's "double victim." Has he ever confessed to what he's done? No. Do his past actions still rob my peace? Not in the least.

4. Is there an enemy you should be praying for?

CHAPTER FOURTEEN

Although there are prophetic references to his appearance, it's interesting the only physical description of Jesus Christ in the Gospels is when he's in his glorified state—a glory so intense that in the book of Revelation when one of his closest friends sees him, the friend does a face plant, counting himself as good as dead. God's presence demands nothing but our greatest reverence—and yet he wants us to enjoy his deepest intimacy.

I've only had one encounter with Christ. It was terrifying. His brightness and glory were overwhelming. And yet, when he spoke, it was with the kindest and most gentle voice I've ever heard. What an amazing paradox—God who is not either/or, but Who is both—blazing, unapproachable glory—and gentle, beckoning tenderness.

1. How do we approach God as both ruler of the Universe and most intimate of friends? For what it's worth, during my quiet whispers to him throughout the day, I often address him as, "My King and Friend . . ." How do you handle the paradox?

As Will struggles with what he feels is an impossible request, Yeshua explains there is a difference between Will's *"I can'ts"* versus his *"I won'ts."* Once again it seems we've returned to free will.

2. To what extent do you believe Paul's claim in Philippians 4:13, *"I can do all things through him who gives me strength"*? What areas do you confuse *"I can't"* with *"I won't"*?

Yeshua suggests Will do only what he can and trust God to do the rest. In Mark 9, Jesus asks a father if he believes he can heal his demon-possessed son. The man cries out, "I believe, help me overcome my unbelief!" The father has enough faith to come to Jesus but not enough to get the job done. He does only what he can do—and Jesus honors that by doing the rest.

That's why Hebrews 12:2 is such a comfort when it refers to Jesus as not only the "pioneer" of my faith but also its "perfecter." All I have to give him is all I have. If it's only some kid's lunch, he'll use it to feed thousands.

Finally, we see Will once again complaining that it's easier to follow religious formulas than to have a relationship.

3. How is this true? How is it false?

4. What situations cause you to resort to rules instead of relationship?

CHAPTER FIFTEEN

Like many people, one of my favorite movies is, *It's a Wonderful Life*. So many Kingdom truths about how it's the little, unnoticed acts that are often the most eternal. One moment I always find moving is when our hero is at the end of his rope and prays for God's help in a bar. And his answer? One of the patrons punches him in the face and then he is thrown out into the snow. One time or another, haven't we all received that or something similar as our answer?

I understand part of that is the enemy testing our faith. But I think there's more. And I think it comes down to God loving us more than we love ourselves. We want an aspirin to mask the pain. God wants to permanently remove the disease so it never torments his child again.

In our story, Will finally steps out and exercises his faith by praying. Instead of the answer he wants, he gets a punch in the face.

1. Can you think of a specific time you put it all on the line for God and he let you down?

In some cases, the work he's doing is so deep we won't understand it for months, years, decades. Sometimes it's so eternal we'll never know this side of heaven. And that's where relationship comes in—knowing someone so well you trust them, regardless.

2. When your child was younger, were there times you wanted to make their life fuller but because you knew they wouldn't understand the cost, you held off—even though it would have been for their best?

Yet, as the child matured and their trust in you grew, you were able to introduce those deeper, more powerful aspects of love.

3. Are there times you simply cannot explain why God has let you down?

4. Has it weakened your trust in him?

5. Outside of making God explain himself, how can that trust be rebuilt?

CHAPTER SIXTEEN

Besides a display of his awesome power, two things always move me about Jesus raising Lazarus from the dead.

First—the timing:

How confused I would have been as a disciple (and outraged as a sister) to know Jesus deliberately lagged behind as the situation grew worse. Not only worse, but hopeless—as in dead and buried. God not only waited until the last minute, he showed up four days later.

But, if I knew Christ had something even greater planned, wouldn't I have been willing to go the distance with him? Seems we're back to trust and faith. Not the type I can work up on my own but the type that comes from really knowing him. It's interesting how Jesus didn't do this with strangers but with his close, trusted friends. As if the reward for greater friendship is greater testing, leading to greater faith, leading to greater character—transforming us from toddlers, barely able to walk, to Olympian track stars.

It seems that's always the bottom line—God being more concerned about our eternal character than our momentary circumstance.

1. Instead of praying for God to meet our timetables (no matter how logical they seem), what would happen if we not only accepted his schedule, but actually worshiped and thanked him for it?

Suddenly, we'd no longer be praying against God but praying *with* him, freeing him up to do his greatest will.

The second thing that moves me about this story is God's compassion. Jesus knew full well what he was going to do. And yet he's as emotionally wrecked as the sisters—not because he doubts what he's about to accomplish but because he shares their pain.

What a comfort to know that even as the Master Surgeon performs surgery deep in my soul, he is relating to my pain and confusion. No, he's not relating. He's in there aching with me.

CHAPTER SEVENTEEN

I love the honesty of the Psalms. If the author is frustrated at what God is doing, he says it. There's no covering up his emotions with religious platitudes. Granted, since he's dealing with truth, the writer eventually gets around to acknowledging God is good and in control—but he doesn't always start there.

The point is—if God is our God, then he's God of our emotions as well as our minds. Hiding what we're feeling may actually prevent him from getting to the real issue. It would be like suffering great pain and going to the doctor saying, "Nope, everything's all right, I'm fine." Before the cure, we have to acknowledge the symptoms to find the disease.

1. In your life, are there secret areas of resentment toward God? What is preventing you from discussing them with him?

Moving on.

I take Jesus's claims of being the Bread of Life very seriously. Ever since I was in high school, I've tried to carve out a little time each morning to feed upon him. There is no single habit in my life more impactful. We feed our bodies three times a day, often with a few snacks thrown in. How often do we feed our souls? Once a week in church? Can you imagine what would happen to our bodies if we fed them as seldom as we feed our souls?

"But I haven't the time," friends say. Sorry, no sale. We manage to find time to feed our bodies which are only temporary. What would happen if we committed to treat our eternal souls with the same care and respect?

2. What is preventing you from daily feeding upon Christ? If you are seriously motivated, what practical steps can you take to change that?

Finally, I was repulsed at writing the section on the bull sacrifice. How brutal and disgusting. But as I worked on it, I became less sickened at God's solution for removing sin and more aware of sin's powerful ugliness. Sin is not a minor indiscretion, not some bill Jesus shrugs over and pays. It's so monstrous it called for the brutal and disgusting murder of innocent animals. So evil it called for the inhumane slaughtering of God.

3. Are there any "minor" sins in your life you've grown use to, made accommodations for?

CHAPTER TWENTY-ONE

The climax of this scene is inspired from a vision Graham Cooke once had. He was sitting on a hillside filled with condemnation over a failure when he saw Jesus approaching up the hill. But instead of a kind, loving face, Cooke saw the Lord angry and heard him demanding over and over again to, "Give me back my stuff." Cooke was shocked and confused and kept asking, "What stuff do you mean?" Until Jesus finally replied, "All that stuff I paid for. That's my stuff. I bought it with all my suffering. I paid for it with my life. Give it back to me!"

What a reversal of thought—believing we're somehow more godly by hanging on to our guilt (and suffering over it) instead of handing it all over. Of course, this is no excuse to sin. In chapter 17 we caught a minor glimpse of how deadly sin is. And there's nothing wrong with repenting in tears. But once we're through, once we've handed it over to Jesus, it's his, not ours. Allowing ourselves to continue feeling broken and dirty, even a little, is not noble or holy. It's simply stealing Christ's glory.

That said:

1. Are there areas in your life where you feel God is still holding a grudge against you?

2. Do you really believe he considers you absolutely perfect?

3. Do you believe he loves you as much as his own Son (John 17:20–23)?

4. If not, what is the remedy so you can give Christ his fullest glory?

CHAPTER TWENTY-TWO

How would you live differently if . . .

1. Life's purpose is not to reach a destination, but to become changed during the journey.

2. The process (how you're struggling with an issue) is more important than the final product?

3. Difficulties are actually Father/child projects designed for us to work side by side with God—getting to know him more deeply as we learn how he views and handles situations—preparing us to be co-heirs and co-rulers with his Son.

4. God is always at your side, even when you fall. And when you fall, he can hardly wait for you to let him help you back on your feet to continue journeying with him into holiness.

A sample from the brilliant follow-up to
Rendezvous with GOD
Volume One

RENOVATION

Rendezvous with GOD
Volume Two

THERE WERE ABOUT a dozen of them—angry men encircling him, shoving him along the edge of a cliff. They held both his arms, shouting to one another, and screaming into his face, "We know your brothers, your mother! Son of a whore!"

I worked my way in closer. As always, no one could see or hear me. Except Yeshua. And, when our eyes finally connected, everything stopped. Not entirely, but everyone began moving in slow motion. *Very* slow motion. Their anger was still present, their mouths still opened in shouts and oaths, but their voices were barely audible—just faint, low rumblings. Except for Yeshua.

"Hey there," he said. "It's been a while." He didn't smile but he definitely didn't look as concerned as he should be.

"Uh . . ." as usual I was at a loss for words, ". . . impressive."

He leaned past a shouting face to better see me. "Time's a relative thing, remember?"

I nodded. It wasn't the first time I saw him defy the laws of physics. Nor was it the first time I saw him irritate people. I motioned to the surrounding mob. "Still not great at making friends, I see."

He broke into that smile of his. "Man's pride, God's truth—not always a good combo."

I pushed in closer, ducking under an upraised fist frozen in the air. "And this doesn't bother you? People hating you like this?"

He glanced around and sighed. "Not my first choice. But . . ."

"But what?"

"My identity is not wrapped up in what other people think of me."

I sensed a lesson coming and I wasn't wrong. "Are we talking about what happened back on campus?"

"You're still letting other people determine your value. You keep seeing yourself through their lens."

"And the right lens is . . . ?"

"God's. The One seeing you as his loved son."

I scoffed. "Easy for you to say."

"Why is that?"

"You *are* his loved son."

"And so are you." I turned to him. Those golden-brown eyes focused on mine. "You have no idea how much we adore you, do you?"

I glanced away, cleared my throat. "I think I saw that up on the hill, when you were being tortured to death."

"And who was that for, Will?"

I swallowed and glanced to the ground. He waited for my answer. When I found my voice, it was thick with emotion. "For me—you did it for me."

He didn't respond. I looked up to see him staring off in the distance. Finally, he spoke, "And when I face that day, it will come out of a passion so deep, you'll never be able to fully understand."

"*When* you face it? You already went through it. I saw you." He looked back to me and I had the answer. "Right," I said, "time's a relative thing." I glanced at his hands. There were no scars, not like I'd seen the last time when he was fixing breakfast for his guys on the beach.

He continued, "What you saw on that hill was our love for you. A love valuing your life as greater than mine."

My vision blurred with moisture and I glanced away.

"You have no idea how deeply we cherish you, Will. And that, my friend, is your greatest weakness." I looked up to him as he continued, "If you grasped just a glimmer of our passion then the opinions of others, good or bad, would mean absolutely nothing." He motioned to the surrounding crowd. "Their words would be as indiscernible as they are now." He reached behind my ear and caught a rock slowly floating toward my head.

I looked at it startled, then answered, "But their words, sometimes they're loud and overwhelming."

He nodded, paused to weigh the rock in his hand before answering. "I'll always be with you, though. Always."

I took a deep breath, knowing I should believe him.

He wasn't finished. "But remember, we're only part of the solution."

"Part?" I asked. "And the other is?"

"You."

I scowled, trying to understand. "I thought it was a free ride, that things were supposed to get easier now."

He broke out laughing, then motioned to the crowd. "I'm sorry, does this look easier?"

"But, that's why you came. You're supposed to do the heavy lifting so we don't have to. For your glory, you said."

"No."

"No?"

"Paying for your sins is my glory. Your growth is what we accomplish together. Otherwise, you'd never learn to co-rule with me."

"Wait, what?"

"This next season is going to be tough. You're going to face huge problems. But it's important you face those problems so you can grow with me, so you can learn how to rise above them."

"Wait?" I repeated. "What about prayer? Isn't that supposed to make things easier? Prayer changes things, right?"

"Of course. And the greatest thing it changes is . . ." He waited for my full attention. ". . . *You*. Not your circumstances. Circumstances come and go, but you, your soul, that's what will live forever. That's where our real interest lies."

I paused, thinking it through. "Which is why you don't always answer prayer?"

He shook his head. "We always answer prayer. Just in bigger ways than you expect. Sometimes we use the circumstance to teach, so you can develop and grow until you're bigger than the situation."

"*Teach, develop, grow*. You make it sound like I'm in some sort of training program."

"You are."

I gave him a look.

"But only if you want."

"And if I don't?"

He cocked his head at me as if I knew the answer.

I did. "Free will," I said. "One of your favorite topics."

He nodded. "That's right. But people forget their freedom continues—all the way to the end and beyond."

"Meaning?"

"Too many of my followers choose to quit, remaining infants who will continually soil their diapers." He looked away, sighing wearily. "Still, they're our children and we'll always love them." He focused back on me. "But for those who choose to continue, to agree to become everything the Father and I dreamed they would be before we created them, then yes, they'll be in a training program—and difficult circumstances are part of their development."

"To rule with you," I said, making sure he heard my skepticism.

"And to judge angels."

I opened my mouth, but no words came.

"Now, if you'll excuse me." He reached out and placed the rock in the air where it was before he grabbed it—then moved me a step to the side so it would miss my head. "I need to focus, here. My old friends and neighbors want to show their appreciation for what I said by throwing me over this cliff."

Suddenly, I realized where we were—the angry men, the valley floor below. "Nazareth," I said. "This is your home town, where they tried to kill you?"

"Living out truth isn't always popular but you have my word, if you keep saying yes and stay with the program, you, my good friend, will become whole and complete lacking in nothing."

I could only stare.

"Oh and remember." There was no missing the twinkle in his eyes. "I never play defense."

And with that strange, foreboding encouragement, I was back on the ferry, standing on the deck, preparing for—well—I had no idea.

What's Been Said About Bill Myers's Previous Books

Blood of Heaven

"With the chill of a Robin Cooke techno-thriller and the spiritual depth of a C. S. Lewis allegory, this book is a fast-paced, action-packed thriller." —Angela Hunt, *NY Times* best-selling author

"Enjoyable and provocative. I wish I'd thought of it!" —Frank E. Peretti, *This Present Darkness*

ELI

"The always surprising Myers has written another clever and provocative tale." —Booklist

"With this thrilling and ominous tale, Myers continues to shine brightly in speculative fiction based upon biblical truth. Highly recommended." —*Library Journal*

"Myers weaves a deft, affecting tale." —*Publishers Weekly*

The Face of God

"Strong writing, edgy . . . replete with action . . ." —*Publishers Weekly*

Fire of Heaven

"I couldn't put the *Fire of Heaven* down. Bill Myers's writing is crisp, fast-paced, provocative . . . A very compelling story."
—Francine Rivers, *NY Times* best-selling author

Soul Tracker

"Soul Tracker provides a treat for previous fans of the author but also a fitting introduction to those unfamiliar with his work. I'd recommend the book to anyone, initiated or not. But be careful to check your expectations at the door . . . it's not what you think it is." —Brian Reaves, *Fuse* magazine

"Thought provoking and touching, this imaginative tale blends elements of science fiction with Christian theology."
—*Library Journal*

"Myers strikes deep into the heart of eternal truth with this imaginative first book of the Soul Tracker series. Readers will be eager for more." —*Romantic Times* magazine

Angel of Wrath

"Bill Myers is a genius." —Lee Stanley, producer, Gridiron Gang

Saving Alpha

"When one of the most creative minds I know gets the best idea he's ever had and turns it into a novel, it's fasten-your-seat-belt time. This one will be talked about for a long time."
—Jerry B. Jenkins, author of *Left Behind*

"An original masterpiece." —Dr. Kevin Leman, best-selling author

"If you enjoy white-knuckle, page-turning suspense, with a brilliant blend of cutting-edge apologetics, *Saving Alpha* will grab you for a long, long time." —Beverly Lewis, *NY Times* best-selling author

"I've never seen a more powerful and timely illustration of the incarnation. Bill Myers has a way of making the gospel accessible and relevant to readers of all ages. I highly recommend this book." —Terri Blackstock, *NY Times* best-selling author

"A brilliant novel that feeds the mind and heart, *Saving Alpha* belongs at the top of your reading list." —Angela Hunt, *NY Times* best-selling author

"*Saving Alpha* is a rare combination that is both entertaining and spiritually provocative. It has a message of deep spiritual significance that is highly relevant for these times." —Paul Cedar, Chairman, Mission America Coalition

"Once again Myers takes us into imaginative and intriguing depths, making us feel, think and ponder all at the same time. Relevant and entertaining. *Saving Alpha* is not to be missed." —James Scott Bell, best-selling author

The Voice

"A crisp, express-train read featuring 3D characters, cinematic settings and action, and, as usual, a premise I wish I'd thought of. Succeeds splendidly! Two thumbs up!" —Frank E. Peretti, *This Present Darkness*

"Nonstop action and a brilliantly crafted young heroine will keep readers engaged as this adventure spins to its thought-provoking conclusion. This book explores the intriguing concept of God's power as not only the creator of the universe, but as its very essence." —Kris Wilson, *CBA* magazine

"It's a real 'what if?' book with plenty of thrills . . . that will definitely create questions all the way to its thought-provoking finale. The success of Myers's stories is a sweet combination of a believable storyline, intense action, and brilliantly crafted, yet flawed characters." —Dale Lewis, TitleTrakk.com

The Seeing

"Compels the reader to burn through the pages. Cliff-hangers abound, and the stakes are raised higher and higher as the story progresses—intense, action-shocking twists!" —TitleTrakk.com

When the Last Leaf Falls

"A wonderful novella . . . Any parent will warm to the humorous reminiscences and the loving exasperation of this father for his strong-willed daughter . . . Compelling characters and fresh, vibrant anecdotes of one family's faith journey." —*Publishers Weekly*